WRONG SIDE OF THE CLAW

MYSTIC NOTCH COZY MYSTERY SERIES #7

LEIGHANN DOBBS

SUMMARY

Bookstore owner Willa Chance has no idea that things in Mystic Notch are about to take a turn for the worse.

When a string of robberies escalates to murder, Willa is baffled by the behavior of her sister, the county sheriff. Normally the gung-ho lawwoman would be all over the case, but she seems more interested in doing her nails and picking out jazz music instead.

Willa has no choice but to take it upon herself to investigate. After all, her sister's reputation is at stake, and a killer is running loose around town. Plus she has a secret weapon—she can see ghosts. Talking to the spirit of a murder victim usually helps solve the case, but not this time. This ghost seems reluctant to help Willa out. Even her boyfriend, neighboring county sheriff Eddie Striker, can't get the spirit of the victim to give them a straight answer.

But things are even worse than they seem. Pandora and the cats of Mystic Notch know the real reason behind the crime goes a lot deeper than robbery or even murder.

Someone has evil plans for Mystic Notch, and the cats need Willa's help to stop them.

With Gus out of commission and the cats struggling to stop the town's most notorious feline from gaining the upper hand, the future of Mystic Notch is in jeopardy. It's going to take a lot of magic to set things right—are Willa and Pandora up for the task?

1

Late fall in the quaint town of Mystic Notch was normally quite picturesque. The distant mountains, blanketed in the reds, oranges, and yellows of the turning leaves, provided the perfect backdrop for the white spires of the First Hope Church. Flowering mums in vibrant shades of purple, crimson, gold, and orange overflowed from the large planters that lined Main Street, adding a perfect complement to the old brick buildings that housed the shops and businesses. The crisp, fresh air, warmed by sunshine during the day, cooled to almost frosty temperatures at night. It was usually one of my favorite times of year.

But not *this* year.

This year it was overshadowed by the string of robberies that had plagued my sleepy little town. Now, instead of feeling joy at the shop windows under their bright awnings, I felt trepidation, wondering who would be next.

Pandora, my cat, must have shared my feelings. I could tell by the way she was sticking to the middle of the sidewalk instead of skulking around the edges near the buildings, where her gray fur would blend into the shadows, giving her an advantage over a poor, unsuspecting wren or chickadee.

I, too, was staying clear of the door openings and dark alleys. Silly, I knew—it was only a string of break-ins. It wasn't like people were being murdered. In fact, nothing had even been stolen.

Though I knew some of the shop owners were nervous, the robberies hadn't put off tourists. No sense in wasting time worrying about it, I thought. Pulling my gray-and-white striped cardigan closer around me, I headed toward Last Chance Books, the shop I'd inherited from my beloved grandmother. Her passing was what had brought me to Mystic Notch several years ago. Well, that and the fact I'd needed time and space to recover from the car accident that had injured my leg. The leg was nearly back to normal now, but as winter neared, I still got twinges in it. I also got twinges when I walked too fast, like now. Cringing, I slowed my pace. Overdoing it would cause more pain, but if I took it easy on myself, the leg would stop hurting.

We passed Buckley's Candy Store, and I glanced in to

make sure everything looked as it should. It was closed since it was still early, but the displays were all in the right place. Good, no break-in there last night.

A few shops down, the local knitting shop, A Good Yarn, was open. Mrs. Quimby, the proprietor, glanced out the window at me and waved. She was quite elderly now, and I was concerned for her, especially in light of the break-ins. I thought about stopping to check on her, but she looked fine, and I was already running a bit late, so I waved back and continued on, making a note to myself to call her later, when things weren't so hectic.

A few stores down, I could see my regulars had already congregated at the door of Last Chance Books. They had their usual Styrofoam coffee cups in hand and were looking down the street toward me expectantly. I suppose one could say I'd inherited them from my grandmother along with the store and Pandora. The senior citizens had been gathering at the bookstore first thing in the morning to discuss town gossip with Gram for decades, and who was I to end the tradition? Besides, they were charming and good company.

"Morning, Willa," Bing Thorndike greeted me as I paused to unlock the thick oak door. He passed me one of the coffees he'd been holding and gave me a kindly smile while holding the door I'd just opened so everyone could file in. A magician in his younger days, Bing still had a magical aura about him, even though he'd retired years ago.

Pandora trotted in alongside me, her kinked tail held high. I flipped on the lights and stashed my purse under the front counter. The bookstore was located in an old mill building and retained much of the décor of its former incarnation—lots of brick and wood. I took a deep breath, savoring the earthy vanilla-tinged scent of old paper that lingered in the air. Aisle after aisle of books filled the space along with scattered sitting nooks for reading or quiet socializing.

The regulars had taken their seats on the purple microsuede sofa and chairs near the front of the store. Bing sat in one of the chairs, and Josiah Barrows, the retired postmaster, in another. The octogenarian twins, Hattie and Cordelia Deering, sat next to each other on one of the sofas as they usually did. Today, Cordelia was wearing a pastel-green suit with a buttercup-yellow shirt beneath, and Hattie was wearing a buttercup-yellow suit with a pastel-green shirt beneath. I guess they still hadn't gotten the memo that fall had arrived—the colors seemed far more appropriate for Easter than November, but then, Hattie and Cordelia did walk to the beat of their own drum.

"Have you heard any more about the break-ins from Gus?" Hattie asked me after sipping her coffee.

Gus, short for Augusta, was my sister and also the town sheriff.

"No." I took my coffee behind the counter and started to get ready to open for the day by counting out the register drawer from the night before. "You know she doesn't talk shop with me."

That was an understatement. Not only did Gus not talk shop with me, she became very angry when I tried to "butt in"—as she called it—to her investigations. She'd even threatened me with jail time on a few occasions. A little drastic if you ask me. I mean, I'd only been trying to help. Gus took the solving of crimes in Mystic Notch very seriously, and allowing amateurs to help was just not on her agenda.

"I'd think she might make an exception with these, though," Bing said. "Considering they could affect your livelihood as well."

Pandora had been making her way around the group, collecting her obligatory pets. She stopped at Bing, and it almost looked as though she nodded up at him. He smiled back. Weird behavior, but I'd seen it between the two of them before. Pandora glanced back at me then trotted to her plush cat bed in the window and settled in.

"How many burglaries have there been now?" Josiah asked.

"Three," I said. "In the past two weeks."

"Gosh," Cordelia said, shaking her head. "What is

this town coming to? Crimes never happen in Mystic Notch."

"If you don't count the murders," Bing said.

Pandora meowed as if in agreement.

"What about that cute Eddie Striker?" Hattie gave me a knowing look over the top of her turquoise reading glasses. "Surely you two aren't keeping any secrets from each other."

"No." Heat prickled my cheeks as I thought of Striker. We'd been spending a lot of time together this past year, and the recent discovery that we both had a peculiar talent for seeing ghosts had brought us even closer together. Striker was the sheriff in the neighboring county, and Gus sometimes called him in to help on cases. He had a lot more experience investigating murder cases than she did, and with the rash of suspicious deaths that had happened in the last year or so, his help had been much appreciated. "He doesn't know anything official about what's going on here, though. Gus hasn't asked for his help."

"They're not technically burglaries, from what I hear," Bing said, jarring me out of my thoughts. "According to the owners, nothing was taken."

"That's odd," Cordelia said.

"But it's happened at three different stores." Hattie played with the plastic lid of her Styrofoam coffee cup. "Doesn't that seem weird to anyone else?"

"Sure does," Josiah said. "What do you think the person is after?"

Bing's expression turned serious. "We don't know that they're after anything. Maybe they are just not that good at stealing, or it's kids on a lark."

"Or the shop owners could be making it up," Hattie suggested. "You know, for the insurance money."

"I don't think that's the case," Josiah said. "They haven't claimed anything was stolen, and why would Bernie put a new lock in the lamp shop if he'd made the whole thing up?"

"Yeah, I saw Deena down at the hairdresser's, and she was very upset about the break-in at her curio shop," Cordelia said. "Didn't seem like she was making it up. You know Deena. Her ears turn all red when she lies, and her ears were as white as a sheet."

"It still leaves some strange questions, though." Josiah tipped the cup to get the last sip of coffee. "Because why would someone break into a shop and not take anything?"

* * *

PANDORA SHIFTED in her bed so that the sun was shining directly on her while the humans talked over on the sofa. She wanted them to think she was sleeping, even though she wasn't. She had one eye closed and the other watching across the street where a lone leaf was losing its battle to cling to the branch of the oak tree in front of the store. Birds chirped from nearby, and a squirrel stuffed his cheeks with acorns, rushing up and down the block, gathering food for the winter.

Beneath all the talk in the bookstore, Pandora could feel the energy of the two ghosts who inhabited the space, Robert Frost and Franklin Pierce. They were more a nuisance than anything, if you asked her. The one was always spouting off his boring poetry while the other grumbled about the incorrect histories written about him. Pandora couldn't care less about either of them. They never petted her or gave her treats, and neither said a word of praise about the true hero there, the cat. But her former human, Willa's grandmother Anna, had been fond of them, and Willa seemed to have developed a certain rapport with them, so Pandora tolerated their presence.

Truth be told, Pandora was far more worried about the break-ins than any of the humans. She knew that stealing from the stores had never been the purpose of the crimes to begin with. At least not according to the gang of cats she hung around with. Rumor had it the break-ins had a much more sinister purpose, one that could change the happy, peaceful vibe of Mystic Notch into one of toxic bickering and hate.

According to feline lore, a pleasantry charm had

been cast on Mystic Notch nearly three hundred years ago by accused witch Hester Warren. The charm ensured that things in town were always pleasant, people worked together, neighbors helped neighbors. It was a protection against the evil element that was always trying to rear its ugly head.

The charm had a variety of ingredients associated with it, and Hester had scattered those in various hiding places around town as a protection against evil. There was only one way to reverse the charm, and that involved collecting all the ingredients. And if someone who didn't want things to be so pleasant anymore managed to collect them all... Pandora shuddered to think what might happen.

Legend said that Hester wrote down the locations in a document that she passed on to her granddaughter. A few months back, that document had resurfaced but had been shredded and scattered to the four winds before anything terrible happened.

That was what the cats had hoped for, anyway. But if it hadn't, and someone had found the pieces and reassembled them, then... things would not be good.

No. As part of the coven of the ancient cats of Mystic Notch, it was her job, along with some of the other cats in town, to ensure those ingredients were never found. They needed to keep a close eye on this situation and on one disagreeable feline in particular, a large white

Persian named Fluff. Fluff and his human, Felicity Bates, were at the root of these break-ins. Pandora would swear to it. She'd also heard that Fluff had recently found part of the ingredients list. If that wasn't a recipe for trouble, Pandora didn't know what was.

As if on cue, Fluff came strolling down the block on the other side of the street with Felicity. He was wearing that ridiculous-looking pink harness and had his poofy tail held high, oozing feline arrogance. Pandora hissed low. No self-respecting cat would be caught dead walking on a leash like that. It was humiliating, not to mention silly looking. Then again, his human wasn't exactly known for her subtlety and good taste. Felicity's high heels clickety-clacked along beside him. Her outfit was silly, too, a flowing psychedelic-patterned thing that clashed with her long red hair. The two of them together spelled bad news, with a capital B.

Felicity Bates claimed openly to be a witch. Pandora stretched and sighed. If she was one, she was not very good. If she did get her hands on those ingredients and tried to reverse the charm, the results could be dire. Not that Felicity would care. She'd had it out for the good folks of Mystic Notch for years. Rumor amongst the cats of the town was that Fluff did her dirty work, so maybe he'd been searching for the ingredients for his master.

Speaking of the local cat gang, she needed to hold another meeting with them in Elspeth's barn to discuss current events. Tonight Pandora would take a trip over to see them. It had been a few days since their gang had convened, and with luck, someone else had some new information to share as well.

Behind Pandora, the humans finished their coffees and conversation and began to leave. They were all laughing and talking as they exited out onto the street, waving to one another as they went their separate ways. Pandora wasn't one to get too sentimental over trivial humans, but the thought of these people coming to harm because the pleasantry charm had been reversed was unsettling, to say the least.

Pandora rolled over to face the interior of the store. Willa was putting away books now, humming as she made her way around the store. At first, Pandora hadn't been sure about Willa, but over time, she'd become attached to her new human. She tried to communicate with Willa telepathically, the same way she did with Bing, but so far it was hit or miss. It would be easier if Willa was a believer, of course, but one couldn't have everything.

Even though Willa wasn't the brightest of humans, she was still the blood relative of Pandora's dear Anna, and Pandora couldn't stand the thought of anything happening to Willa because of the charm being reversed.

Meow. Nothing would happen, because Pandora wouldn't let it. She turned her attention back to Felicity and Fluff, who had made their way down the street. They passed Gus, who appeared to be on her way to the bookstore. The two women nodded at each other, and Pandora's whiskers twitched. As far as she knew, Gus and Felicity hated each other. But the nods they gave seemed awfully cordial. Pandora's fur ruffled with suspicion.

What was *that* about?

2

M y sister, Gus, sidled into the bookstore mere seconds after the others had left. I checked the clock and sighed. Time to officially open for the day.

"Hey, Willa," Gus called as I walked to the front to flip the sign in the window. "Got any books on piano jazz?"

"Piano jazz?" I scrunched my nose and gave her a skeptical look. I knew Gus played piano at the Blue Moon sometimes, but she never liked to talk about it. "You looking for some new tunes to play?"

"Something like that." Gus wandered off into the stacks, leaving me to stare after her. She looked different today, more relaxed. Usually, Gus did her level best to look as professional as possible to counteract what nature had given her. Growing up, I remember people were constantly comparing her to a Barbie doll—with her petite hourglass shape and long blond hair. Only thing she didn't have were the big blue eyes. Gus's were amber-colored instead, a gift from our mother. Physically, we looked nothing alike since I was taller and willowier. The only characteristic we shared was our eyes.

Gus normally wore her hair pulled back into a tight bun, I assumed to make herself look more severe and, therefore, garner more respect as the county sheriff. Today she wore it down, and it cascaded over her shoulder like a golden waterfall. It didn't look bad, just... different.

"Have you found out anything more about the break-ins?" I asked, straightening the area where the regulars had been earlier. "People are worried."

Gus poked her head around the end of a bookshelf and shrugged. "Not really. Don't see why it's such a big deal anyway. It's not like anything went missing."

Confused at her relaxed attitude, I walked over to where she was sorting through the volumes, humming a tune I'd not heard before. "So, you're saying burglaries aren't a top priority for the Mystic Notch Sheriff's Department?"

"No." Gus gave me an annoyed glance. "What I'm saying is I'd really like to learn a few new piano tunes for my next gig down at the Blue Moon lounge."

Weird. My sister had never been so cavalier before

about crimes in her town, nor had she been forthcoming about information when I'd asked her about cases. Her usual response was for me to butt out. Today, though, it seemed she couldn't care less.

"Why?" Gus straightened, a book on the music of the late Miles Davis in her hand. "You got any leads for me to follow up on, sis?"

"Uh, no." My confusion mounted. She'd never been interested in any of my leads regarding one of her cases before. Just the opposite. On most days, Gus brimmed with warning about staying away from anything she was working on.

"What about drinks?"

"Drinks?"

"Yeah. You got any books on mixing drinks?" Gus asked. "Specifically, drinks that were popular back in the 1920s?"

"I don't think so." I walked down another aisle of shelves, Gus trailing behind me. "I've got a couple of bartending books in stock but nothing focusing on that time period. Sorry."

"Can you order one for a bartender friend?"

"Probably. If you have a specific book name, then I have a database I can search." We walked up to the register, and Gus paid for the Miles Davis book. "Want a bag for that?"

"Nah. I'll get back to you on the bartending book."

Gus smiled and headed for the front door. "See you around, sis."

Weird. That whole encounter had been odd, like something out of *The Twilight Zone*. I leaned back against the counter and pulled out my phone. Maybe there was something going on at the sheriff's department. I quickly typed in a text to Striker to see if he'd heard anything.

He responded a few minutes later, saying he hadn't and asking what was wrong.

I told him she just wasn't acting like her usual crime-fighting self.

His response that he would stop by my sister's office later and check it out made me feel all warm and fuzzy.

With a sigh, I shut my phone off and settled in for a long morning of bookkeeping. I'd just pulled out one of the ledgers when Pandora wandered over and began meowing loudly. It almost felt like she was trying to tell me something. The same thing had happened a couple of times since I'd become her owner, these weird human-feline vibes where it seemed she was doing her best to push a message into my mind, but I just never got it. Maybe if I concentrated really hard...

My focus was broken by another customer coming in, an older lady looking for a copy of *Trixie Belden: The Secret of the Mansion*. I got her rung up then looked back at Pandora again, only to be interrupted by my best friend, Pepper St. Onge. She waltzed in, looking adorable as ever with her long red hair and cute plaid skirt and matching sweater in earthy fall colors. Pepper always knew how to dress. My wardrobe, on the other hand, consisted mostly of T-shirts and jeans smudged with dust from crawling around in attics and basements, looking at old books.

Pepper owned the Tea Shoppe a few doors down, and she'd brought fresh scones and tea in the custom quilted bag she had made just for carrying her wares. My stomach rumbled in anticipation of our daily snack, and we settled on the sofas up front so I could keep an eye on the register.

"How's it going today?" she asked as she laid everything out on the coffee table like we were having high tea. I was always amazed at how much she could carry in her bag and watched in awe as she produced everything from a silver teapot to a hand-painted china platter to embroidered napkins. Soon the shop was filled with the scent of oolong tea and strawberry scones.

"Good. Strange." I told her about Gus's visit and the rumors about the break-ins. "And she had her hair down too. I don't think I've ever seen her wear it in anything other than a bun since I came back to town."

"That is weird," Pepper said around a bite of strawberry scone before dabbing her mouth delicately with a napkin. "Oh, before I forget, can you do me a favor later?"

"Of course," I said, sipping my lemon tea. "What is it?"

"I made some new herbal tea mixtures for Elspeth. Would you mind dropping them off at her place tonight on your way home?"

"Absolutely."

"Thanks." Pepper finished her scone then sat back, her expression turning serious. "You know, I've begun to wonder if those break-ins don't have something to do with that list I told you about before. The one with the ingredients to reverse the pleasantry charm."

"Seriously?" I shook my head. Pepper had mentioned something about a list of magical ingredients that could wreak some havoc on the town. I loved my friend, but sometimes she got a bit too fanciful in her thinking. "Old wives' tale, if you ask me. Besides, whatever was on that piece of paper is long gone. I saw the pieces fly away myself."

"Hmm. Maybe." Pepper didn't look convinced. She'd always been a believer in magic. Then again, she'd stayed in Mystic Notch her whole life, and there were enough inexplicable events around here to make a person question the existence of the supernatural. That was true. She even claimed her teas had magical properties, almost like potions. The thought had me glancing at my cup. She swore she never put anything in the tea that she gave to me, but maybe I'd only take a few small sips just the same.

We drank our tea in silence for a few minutes, my mind churning with Gus's odd visit and now the idea that my best friend seemed to think the break-ins might have magical origins. I was still skeptical. Perhaps I shouldn't have been, given the fact I could talk to ghosts. But somehow, talking to ghosts and all the magical things Pepper suggested seemed miles apart. Besides, the goings-on in Mystic Notch had to have a rational explanation.

"I know you have your doubts," Pepper said at last. "But I'm telling you, Willa, something isn't right here. I've got a bad feeling that someone's breaking into these stores to search for those missing ingredients. And if they find them, we're all in trouble."

3

It had been several years since Gram had passed and bequeathed me the old Victorian home in which I had spent so many childhood nights. I had fond memories of myself and Gram in the big white house with its crisp black shutters and detached barn. Pulling into the driveway every night after work gave me a cozy sensation of being home that I'd never felt anywhere else. Even though I'd lived most of my life down in Massachusetts, for some reason, Mystic Notch in general and my grandmother's house in particular were where I now knew I belonged.

Pandora always seemed to get excited when we pulled into the driveway too. Sometimes she would leap across my lap as soon as I opened the driver's-side door of my Jeep and race to the old farmer's porch, then sit at the door, impatiently waiting to be let in. As far as I knew, Pandora had never known any other home. At least I didn't think so. It seemed like my grandmother had owned her for decades. Though I knew that couldn't be right, I actually had no idea how old the cat was but assumed Gram must have gotten a few cats that all looked alike over the years.

I let Pandora in, and she went straight to her bowl in the corner of the old-fashioned kitchen.

"Hungry? I'm starving too," I said as I filled it with dry cat food.

I wasn't kidding either. I'd skipped lunch after eating two of Pepper's scones earlier in the day. Too bad the only things in the fridge were cottage cheese, two jars of olives, and some condiments. I would be the first one to admit that I was not that good at procuring groceries, or cooking for that matter. So I did the next best thing—I texted Striker and asked him to pick up a pizza on his way over.

Honestly, I'd gotten a bit spoiled since we'd been together. He spent nearly every night at my place these days and brought dinner too. It was good we had the evenings together since he'd been so busy during the day fighting crime in Dixford Pass. When he helped Gus out here in the Notch, he would stop by the bookstore often, but these days, he'd been busy in his own county, not that there was much crime there either.

I checked the clock over the stove and saw that I had

just enough time to run Pepper's tea mixture over to Elspeth's place before Striker arrived. I was eager to check up on the elderly woman who had been a second grandmother to me. One of Gram's dying wishes was that I watch over Elspeth, and I intended to honor that. Not that I needed prompting. I was genuinely fond of her.

Night was about to fall, so I exchanged my cardigan for a thick black-and-red-checked flannel jacket and headed out the side door. Pandora must have guessed my intentions because she slipped out alongside me.

Elspeth lived on a street behind my grandmother's house, but there was a path through the woods that led straight between the two houses. I'd traveled it a million times when I was a child.

Twilight was falling earlier and earlier these days, but thankfully the moon was bright enough to light the way through the skeletal tree branches above. If I hadn't known this path so well, it would've been spooky. Pandora trotted along beside me, never veering off course even when we heard the scurrying of chipmunks in the fallen leaves. It was almost as if she had an appointment and didn't want to be late. I knew she liked to hang around with Elspeth's clowder of cats in the barn, but the notion of them actually making plans and having appointments was ridiculous.

We'd walked for about ten minutes when the woods

became less dense and Elspeth's home came into view. Another old Victorian, except hers had a turret in front and was painted mint green with pink gingerbread trim. She also had the most gorgeous climbing roses around her porch that seemed impervious to the cold. Mine were all dead this late in the season, but Elspeth's were still blooming away. She must use some kind of super fertilizer. I would have to ask her for the secret one of these days.

Pandora and I walked up the steps and across the wraparound porch and were greeted by Elspeth's orange tiger cat, Tigger. While I knocked on the front door, Pandora and Tigger sniffed each other in greeting and then took off toward the barn in the back.

Elspeth answered, wearing an apron. Her white hair was braided around her head, and her blue eyes sparkled with intelligence.

"Oh, Willa," she said, inviting me in. "I've been waiting on my tea from Pepper. Come on back to the kitchen, where I'm working."

Elspeth's old-fashioned kitchen always brought a flood of happy childhood memories, and today was no exception. The air smelled of cinnamon and sugar from the freshly baked snickerdoodles on the counter, and the yellow curtains that framed the backyard gave the room a cheery appearance.

I handed her the packet of tea. To me it just looked

like a bunch of crushed-up leaves and twigs, but Elspeth made a big deal about it, placing it carefully on the butcher-block table in the center of the space, as if it were of extreme importance. On the table, a cookbook called *Betty's Recipes* lay open. Huh. The last time I'd seen that book, I'd been led to believe it wasn't so much for concocting food as for conjuring spells. At least that's what Pepper had implied. But seeing as Elspeth was using it to make cookies, that was apparently another one of Pepper's fanciful stories.

"I do hope your bookstore hasn't been affected by those break-ins downtown," Elspeth said, bustling around the room. "I'd hate for anything to happen to you here."

Here I'd come to make sure that Elspeth was okay, and she was more concerned about me. It was just like her to worry about others over herself.

I wanted to put her at ease. "No, no. Everything's fine, Elspeth. Please don't worry on my account. I'm sure Gus will find the culprit soon enough. Even if she is acting a bit weird."

"Weird how?" Elspeth peeled more cookies off the baking sheet with her spatula and plopped them onto a cooling rack.

"Oh, she's just not investigating with her usual zeal." I tried to sound nonchalant. It wouldn't do to get Elspeth all worried about the effectiveness of Mystic Notch's law enforcement. I probably should have kept my big mouth shut about Gus in the first place, but worry over my sister's behavior had made the words spill out of my mouth before I could stop them.

"Huh." Elspeth frowned. "She's not sick, is she? The flu's been going around."

"Oh, I'm sure she'll be okay. You know Gus. She's hardy as a bull moose."

Elspeth gestured for me to sit then brought the plate of cookies over to the table. She smiled as I bit into the sugary confection, but I could see that she was still worried.

"Yes, she hardly ever gets sick. That's what is so worrisome." Elspeth glanced back at the butcher-block table.

I put my hand on her arm. "Don't worry. I'm sure everything will be fine, and besides, we have Striker to fill in if Gus really is sick."

Elspeth brightened at the mention of Striker. "Of course, dear. We are in good hands with him. But still I think we might want to keep our eye on Gus. We wouldn't want her to catch something that would put her out of commission, now would we?"

THE CATS WERE GATHERED in the barn. Some were

perched on tall bales of hay. Others peered down from the loft. There was no lighting in the barn, and they looked like four-legged shadows with bright eyes reflecting in the pale moonlight that streamed in from where the sliding door was cracked open. The scent of hay and roses lingered in the chilly air inside the barn. Pandora could see her own breath form wisps of condensation in front of her.

Inkspot sat in the middle of the barn, the shaft of moonlight highlighting his sleek midnight-black fur as the cats slowly gathered in a circle around him. He was larger than the other cats. His size and striking yellow eyes demanded attention and left no question as to his role as leader. His deep voice boomed through the shadows. "So, we convene again about this list. Pandora, what's your report?"

Pandora hopped up onto a bale of hay and spoke. "I'm telling you, there's something going on with Fluff and that human of his. If I had to guess, I'd say he somehow got his paws on part of the list and shared it with Felicity. If you could've seen her this morning, strutting through town. It was shameful."

"I'll tell you what's shameful," Otis, a persnickety calico, said, his words dripping with sarcasm. "Allowing yourself to be placed in a pink harness and shackled to a human like some kind of dog."

Gasps and meows rang out from the cats.

"Well, I say if Pandora is suspicious, we go with it," Kelly, the Maine coon, said as she flicked her fluffy tail. "Her instincts are rarely wrong."

"Harrumph," Otis hissed. "I don't know if I'd say *rarely*. Though I suppose she has been right a few times."

Pandora narrowed her gaze at Otis. He liked to act superior because he was a very rare cat. Most calicos were female, and he liked to flaunt the fact that he was one of only three percent who were male. Even more than that, though, he seemed to have taken a disliking to Pandora and had been a thorn in her side since day one. Always trying to pick a fight.

She'd thought they'd formed a truce of sorts after a little incident with a potion. Now she wasn't sure. She caught his gaze, and he winked. Winked? Was he simply trying to keep up appearances? Maybe he didn't want the other cats to think he'd gone soft. Pandora decided to ignore his earlier jab. She knew for a fact that when it came down to it, she could count on him to do the right thing, and that was all that mattered.

"Well, we all know that Fluff and his human want to ruin things for everyone, so I say Pandora is probably right," Truffles, a small tortoiseshell cat with greenish-yellow eyes, said.

"Agreed." Snowball flicked her fluffy white tail at Otis. "Plus, I've heard that Felicity Bates has been digging around again, snooping for ingredients."

"Maybe she is the one behind all these break-ins," Truffles said.

"I wouldn't put it past her." Sasha looked up from grooming her paws, her blue eyes glowing in the dark. "Never trusted that human."

"Me neither." Hope, their resident two-faced Chimera cat, sat atop a bale of hay. Of all the cats, Hope had the most unusual markings. Half her face was black with a blue eye, and the other half, orange-striped with a golden eye. But her appearance wasn't the only thing unusual about her. Hope was special, and she and Pandora had a particular bond that went back to a time when Pandora had helped rescue Hope from Fluff's evil clutches.

"Did anything else happen, Pandora?" Inkspot asked.

"As a matter of fact, it did. My human's sister, Gus, came into the bookshop this morning." Pandora stretched and sat up to look down on the others. "She was acting very strangely. Wasn't interested at all in investigating the break-ins."

"Not investigate?" Tigger asked. "But without her handling things on the human side, our jobs will be harder."

"It's true," said Inkspot. "We can lead them to the clues, but it's up to them to make an arrest and imprison the perpetrators."

"I know. I don't like this at all," Pandora said. "Worse

still, I saw Felicity and Gus nodding to each other, like they were in cahoots. This can't bode well."

"I agree. Maybe Gus is just a little under the weather." Inkspot stood, his whiskers twitching with the seriousness of the situation. "But I think we need to keep a close eye on Gus to know for sure. Felicity too. She's sneaky, and we have no idea what she's up to at this point. And we all need to be extra wary now. If the humans are no longer investigating properly, then all manner of evil could take place. They have no idea of the danger they are up against."

4

"I'm telling you, it was just weird. She's not usually so nice to me," I said to Striker later as we sat in my living room, devouring a pepperoni pizza. "And it's certainly not like her to tell me to follow leads."

"That is strange," Striker said, feeding Pandora a slice of pepperoni. "When I stopped by her office earlier, Gus wasn't there. There were notes on her bulletin board, though, about the break-ins, and they looked pretty thorough."

"I don't know. The whole day's been odd." I snuggled closer to his side. We were seated on the couch, the food on the coffee table before us along with our drinks, the TV droning on in the background. Pandora jumped up onto the table and batted at the glass paperweight sitting there.

My gaze fell to the shiny orb as her paw moved it

from one side of the table to the other. I remembered looking into the thing on the last case and seeing... *something*. Not a solution exactly but enough to help me figure out what was going on. It had felt almost magical.

Feeling out of sorts, I leaned forward and picked up the paperweight, looking deep into it. I wasn't sure what I expected to see. It had been a gift from Elspeth when I'd moved back to town, and I was pretty sure it was just a plain old piece of glass she'd gotten down at Deena's Curio Shop. Sure enough, all I saw inside was an upside-down reflection of the room.

So much for magic.

Pandora jumped up to cuddle on the other side of Striker. Couldn't blame the kitty, really. She had excellent taste in men. For his part, Striker made a big show of petting the cat and talking to her like he understood what she was saying.

I laughed and shook my head. "You make it seem like you are really communicating with her."

"I am." He chuckled then kissed the top of my hair. "Well, kind of anyway. We don't talk with words, but you can read their body language. She'll tell you if she's happy or sad or angry or upset."

"Kind of like me, eh?" I leaned up and kissed him.

"Exactly like you." He grinned.

We focused on eating the pizza and making small talk about our day. Honestly, the small talk was my favorite part. I loved hearing about the details of Striker's day, and the way he always seemed interested in mine warmed my heart. After demolishing the pizza, we moved to the kitchen to clean up. We usually traded off on the washing and drying duties. Tonight I was drying.

I turned to Striker. "What should we do about my sister?"

"I don't think we need to do anything." He handed me a washed plate, and I dried it with my red-and-white-striped towel. "I think she is investigating the robberies. I mean, she had it on her board. But honestly, nothing was taken, so what's the urgency? She's probably just bored and taking her time."

"True." I put the plate away and took the next dish from him. "My sister does tend to have a short attention span sometimes."

"Yeah." Striker looked out the window as he washed one of the glasses. "I'll keep an eye on her, but unless something drastic happens, I don't think we have a thing to worry about."

5

———

The next morning, Bing, Hattie, and Cordelia were waiting for me and Pandora at the bookstore as usual. Bing had a cardboard tray with coffees, and I gladly accepted one once I'd unlocked the store and we were all sitting on the sofas.

"Where's Josiah?" I asked, taking a tentative sip of the coffee to test for temperature. It was perfect.

Pandora trotted over, looking a bit agitated. She hopped up on the arm of my chair and pushed her head against my hand. I petted her, but then she hopped down and trotted over to Bing.

"Hello there." Bing smiled down at her, then slowly his smile faded. He and Pandora both glanced toward the door at the same time. Weird.

"He texted me earlier," Bing said. "Told me he was

going to be late. Got his coffee though." He held up the tray with a cup still inside as proof.

"So, any new break-ins?" Cordelia asked. She was wearing a brown suit today under a heavy tan jacket, with a coral-colored blouse. Hattie was dressed the opposite but with an identical tan jacket. At least they were edging closer to season-appropriate colors. "Gus have any new leads?"

Pandora trotted over to Cordelia and meowed.

"No." I told them about her visit the day before. "If she's not making it a priority, then we can't expect an arrest anytime soon either."

The first rays of sunshine streamed in through the front windows of the shop, and my spirits lifted along with the sun. Striker had been right last night. Maybe I was being paranoid. I couldn't help myself, though. I'd been trained as a journalist, and I tended to be suspicious of everything. But that was my old life. I was a bookstore owner now. Those instincts of mine might have been great as a reporter in big-city Boston but not so much as a bookstore owner in a quiet little town in New Hampshire. I should just stop worrying about break-ins and my sister being out of sorts and focus on my own life.

"That's to be expected, I think," Hattie said. "I was having a pedicure yesterday, and Mary Connelly said that talk about the break-ins has died down. No more have happened, and in a few days, I suspect it will be old news."

"That's right, and Gail Greenfield said that there was quite a to-do over the pink flamingos that Joe and Irene Buxton put in their front yard." Cordelia pursed her lips as if the idea of pink flamingo yard ornaments was distasteful. "I suspect that will be the new gossip now."

"I don't know, sister." Cordelia smiled at her twin. "I rather like the flamingos."

"Meow!" Pandora voiced her approval as well.

Bing cleared his throat. "I'm glad there haven't been any further break-ins, but I don't think we should just forget about them." He glanced uneasily at the door. "I mean, I hope Gus is looking into them, though I agree it's not as urgent as if items were stolen."

"Good point," Hattie said. "Next time we might not be so lucky, and the thief could make off with something valuable."

"Or hurt someone," Cordelia added.

We all turned to her, startled by her ominous tone.

"I don't think that will happen. Statistically most thieves don't escalate into harming folks, and this one has been very careful to break into the shops when no one is there," I said.

"Even so, we better—"

"Meow!" Pandora's cry cut off Bing's words. She was over by the door, and as we all turned to look at her, the door burst open, and Josiah ran in, looking flushed and out of breath.

"What's wrong?" Bing asked, standing up and setting the coffees aside. "Calm down before you pass out."

"C-can't," Josiah wheezed, doubling over to rest his hands on his knees.

"What is it? Another break-in?" Cordelia asked.

"No. Worse." Josiah looked up at us, his eyes wide. "There's been a murder!"

6

Josiah collapsed into a chair, and we all gathered around him as he wheezed and coughed. Bing patted him on the back, his expression grim as he glanced up at us. Even Pandora seemed concerned. She sat on the floor at the foot of the chair, her greenish-gold eyes watching us intently.

"It's Jack McDougall," Josiah spit out when he could talk again. "They found him dead in his store just a few minutes ago. Looks like our burglar has escalated from robbery to murder."

"Oh dear!" Cordelia gasped.

"My goodness!" Hattie said.

"Let's see for ourselves." Bing held the door while we all rushed outside. I paused for a few seconds to push Pandora back inside and lock the door. As I started down the street, Pandora hopped into her cat bed in the window and glared at me. I could feel her feline stare burning a hole in my back as I hurried to Jack's Cards, the collectable sports cards store owned by McDougall.

Apparently, we weren't the only ones who wanted a closer look at the crime scene. A small crowd had gathered in front of the store. Jack's wife, Brenda, was standing on the sidewalk, sobbing uncontrollably while Gus's deputy, Jimmy, was doing his best to comfort her. The guy was young and inexperienced, though, and didn't seem to be doing a very good job of it, if Brenda's hysterical wailing was any indication. Her short brown curls bounced around her head each time she shook it.

As we got nearer to the crime scene, I could hear bits of their conversation.

"My husband had stayed overnight to guard the store. You know, because of the break-ins," Brenda said to Jimmy. "I knew something was wrong when he didn't answer his phone this morning. I came down to check and... and... and I found him like that inside. D-dead."

More tears ensued, and who could blame her? Her husband was gone, after all.

I moved in closer with the others, trying to get a glimpse through the front windows of the shop at the scene inside. Not much luck. All I saw was the local medical examiner, an ancient woman named Gertie Sloan, hunched over Jack. His body was on the floor, clear in the back of the store, next to a toppled chair and surrounded by a pool of blood. I wasn't certain, but I guessed it was a gunshot wound based on the hole in the back of the chair.

Gus came outside a moment later and shooed everyone away from the windows. Her demeanor wasn't the take-charge persona she usually had, though. Nope. Today she seemed as laid-back as before, putting her arm around people and personally escorting them from the scene in a friendly manner. Definitely not my sister's normal by-the-book attitude at all. Usually she barked orders and threatened people with jail time if they didn't move along. Still, if her new, kinder attitude meant she might share what she'd learned about what happened with me, I wasn't above schmoozing with her a little.

"Oh darn! We've got a hair appointment," Cordelia said. "Willa, dear. Please let us know what you find out at coffee tomorrow."

Hattie and Cordelia hurried off. I was skeptical about the appointment. My guess was they wanted to be the first ones at the hair salon to announce the morbid news.

"I've seen enough." Josiah turned away. "I'll see you guys later."

Bing and I watched as he headed toward the post office. The former postmasters liked to gather there in the morning, and I imagined this morning he would be sought after like he was a celebrity since he was one of the first on the scene.

Bing stood beside me, glancing first into Jack's store then at the lamp store down the way then over toward the curio shop.

"Do you really think the person behind the break-ins killed Jack?" I asked.

"Seems like there would be a connection, Willa," he said.

"Maybe. It's a big step from break-ins to murder."

"It is. Maybe Jack surprised them, and things got out of hand. Darn shame, though." Bing frowned and shook his head. "I should get home myself." He backed away, hand raised. "See you tomorrow morning, Willa."

"See you." I watched him go then looked around for Gus, thinking I might be able to get some information out of her. She was busy inside the store, though, so I decided it would be wiser to wait until she was free. She probably wouldn't tell me anything, anyway. I was sure this horrible new development would be just the thing that would turn her back into the old Gus.

I headed back to the bookstore, deep in thought. Pepper was waiting for me at the door when I returned. Pandora was still glaring from her cat bed.

"What's happened down there?" Pepper asked, peering at Jack's place in the distance. His building was on the opposite side of the street but a few stores down, so we had to crane our necks to see it from the bookstore window.

I filled her in on what we'd seen then watched out the window with her and Pandora. We spotted Gus leaving the crime scene, looking like she didn't have a care in the world. Poor Jimmy had his hands full, though, trying to keep control of the crowd and console the newly widowed Brenda. My concern over my sister's odd personality shift grew. "I'm telling you, something's wrong with Gus."

"It is strange," Pepper said, gaze narrowed on my sister, who was sauntering off down the street. She looked relaxed as she accepted an iced coffee from Mrs. Q. As the two exchanged a few words, Mrs. Quimby kept glancing uneasily toward Jack's shop. I imagined the older woman was nervous to see the police and medical examiner there, but it looked like Gus was reassuring her, sipping the coffee and patting Mrs. Quimby on the arm.

"I thought maybe Striker was right last night when he said she was bored with her job, but today there's a juicy new murder for her to work with, and she doesn't seem overly interested." I scowled as Gus bid Mrs. Quimby goodbye and started to admire the flowers in one of the large pots under a streetlamp. Normally Gus would never leave a crime scene, wanting to keep control of every little detail.

"Maybe she has a good lead on a suspect?" Pepper suggested. "Perhaps that's why she rushed off."

I raised a brow at her. "That was not a rush, even for a turtle. No. Something's wrong, and I'm going to find out what it is. Besides, a man was killed, and it's not like her to be happy about that. She does have some compassion... or she used to."

"True." Pepper worried her bottom lip, still staring in the direction of Jack's store. "This does not bode well."

"You're thinking about that list again, aren't you?"

"Mew!" Pandora meowed her two cents. The logical side of me still resisted believing in magical lists and hexes, but I had to admit there was something strange about this whole business.

"We can't discount it. I hope there is a logical explanation, though." Pepper glanced out the window one last time then turned away. She reached into the pocket of her jacket and pulled out a pistachio scone. "I brought you this."

"Thanks." Pistachio was one of my favorites, so I bit in right away. It was still slightly warm, as she must have baked it this morning. The sweet almond flavor mixed with the salty pistachio was divine. "It's delicious."

Pepper smiled. "Good. Well, I must get back to the shop. See you later. Let me know if anything develops." She glanced uneasily out the window.

I scarfed down the rest of the scone then called Striker.

"Hey, Willa," he said. "I was just on my way to Jack's Cards. Heard about the murder on the police scanner. I'll stop by if you want."

"Of course." I waited on a customer who walked in just after I ended the call, keeping one eye on the window. I saw Striker's car pass and watched him go inside Jack's store. Gus had wandered back to the scene. That was a good sign, right?

Since the store was empty, and my curiosity was boiling over, I decided to take a stroll down and meet Striker. I locked up the shop amidst Pandora's meows of protest and headed down the street for the second time that morning.

When I arrived at the crime scene, Striker was leaning against the hood of the squad car, beside Gus, who was still sipping her iced coffee.

"Hey," he called to me and waved. His expression was serious, but I couldn't tell if that was because of the gravity of the situation or because Gus was acting like the anti-Gus.

"Hey." I stood next to him and watched the crowd still gathered in front of the store. They'd put up crime-scene tape now at least, I noticed, and it looked like Jimmy had things better under control. I narrowed my gaze at my sister. "Any idea who did this?"

"Nah, not yet," Gus said, looking bored.

"You are investigating though, yes?" Striker asked, arms crossed and expression suspicious.

"Of course. That's my job, right?" Gus shrugged. "You ever listen to jazz, Striker?"

He gave me a side-glance then raised a skeptical brow. "Sure. But I don't see how that has anything to do with Jack's death."

"We'll figure it out. Don't worry." Gus smiled then looked over at the entrance to Jack's Cards, where Gertie was trying to flag her down. "Guess I gotta go. You two take care."

We watched her walk back to the store, iced coffee in hand.

Striker and I headed back to the bookstore in silence. I unlocked the door, and Pandora rushed over to Striker so he could pet her. She purred and rubbed against his ankle, but when I tried to pet her, she skittered out of the way, gave me an angry look, and hopped into her cat bed. I guessed she was still mad I hadn't let her join us when we'd gone down to Jack's earlier. I wasn't worried. I was sure she would get over it with the help of a few of her favorite fish-flavored cat treats.

I turned to Striker. "See? There's something not right with Gus. You can't tell me you didn't notice."

"No. You're right. She's definitely off. Which isn't great, considering there's a killer on the loose."

"Exactly." I slumped back against the counter. "What are we going to do?"

He exhaled slowly. "Well, I have an idea, but I don't think you're going to like it."

"Hey, I'll take anything at this point."

"We get the information directly from the source." Striker made the shape of a ghost with his hands.

My bad leg started to ache. "You mean Jack?"

"Yes. Have you seen him?"

"No. Have you?"

Striker shook his head.

My accident a few years ago had produced another unwanted consequence along with the leg injury. I could see ghosts. Up until recently, the only other person I'd ever told about this was Pepper. Of course she was understanding—maybe even a bit envious—being predisposed to all things magical, and having at least one other person know made it seem less lonely and scary.

I'd hidden the ability from everyone, especially Striker. I hadn't wanted him to think I was weird. Then, by an odd twist of fate, I discovered that Striker could also see ghosts. We couldn't always see the same ghosts, but knowing he had the same, umm... gift was comforting.

Usually I was pestered by ghosts of the recently deceased who wanted me to solve their murders, but Jack hadn't come around with that request yet. Then again, he was newly dead, and it often took ghosts a while to figure out how to communicate. The other thing was that ghosts didn't manifest on command, especially not new ones. New apparitions were more apt to be confused, particularly those like Jack, who had died abruptly.

"Jack might appear in due time, though," Striker suggested.

"But do we have time to wait?" I asked, feeling more discouraged than ever.

"Don't worry, Willa," he said, leaning over to kiss the top of my head. "We'll get 'em. We always do." He straightened and headed for the door. "Got to get back to Dixford Pass. Want to have dinner again tonight?"

I nodded, still preoccupied with the murder.

"Good. I'll see you after work, then." Striker winked at me then left.

He sounded far more optimistic about all this than I felt, but talking to Jack was a good idea, so I locked the shop up and tried to conjure Jack's ghost but only ended up frustrated. From her bed by the front windows, Pandora watched me. I could've sworn she looked amused by my antics.

"It's not that easy, you know," I said to her, grabbing a handful of treats out of the locked filing cabinet. That perked her up. She jumped from her spot on the wide window ledge and landed with a soft meow. I flipped her a few treats then opened up the shop again. "No sense in missing a paying customer."

I had a sinking feeling. Not all ghosts came forward. Some headed straight to the afterlife. I hoped Jack's ghost would at least stick around long enough to tell us what he knew, though with a violent and sudden murder, they often didn't remember much. At least there was one way to know if he was lingering. I could ask my resident ghosts, Franklin Pierce and Robert Frost.

"Franklin? Robert? Are you around?" I called out to the empty shop.

No answer came unless I considered Pandora's snarky meow an answer. She trotted over to the book-shelves, and that gave me an idea. I headed to the history section and knocked one of Pierce's biographies off the shelf to get his attention. At last, an icy cold tingle ran up my arm, signaling Franklin's displeasure. He swirled into existence a moment later.

"How dare you?" he chastised me. "You need to treat literature about me more respectfully."

Robert Frost gave a superior snort. "You'd never see someone knock a book of my poems off the shelf that way."

I did just that to spite him.

"Hey!" Robert's apparition glowered at me. "Careful!"

"Have either of you sensed any new ghosts in Mystic

Notch?" I asked. I didn't have time to beat around the bush.

"Of course," both ghosts answered.

"I'd like to talk to him, please," I said, picking up the fallen books and dusting them off. "The sooner the better."

"Really?" Franklin gave her an inquisitive stare. "That's a change. Usually you try to avoid ghosts as much as possible."

"True." I stuck the books back on the shelf. "But I have questions I need answered from this one, and your kind don't appear on demand. Plus, I think he might be a bit confused."

"Indeed he is," Robert said. "He may be taking the road less traveled."

Franklin rolled his eyes. "Stop with the poem references. The ghost you are seeking has met a violent death, correct?"

"Yep," I said.

Robert and Franklin looked at each other and nodded. At least they knew who I was talking about, but the looks on their faces were not encouraging.

"I'm afraid he is a bit shell-shocked," Robert said.

"He doesn't seem very communicative," Franklin added.

Robert leaned close enough to cause a cold mist on my arm. "Close-lipped."

"We'll see what we can do to get him to contact you," Franklin said, his image already fading. "But don't hold your breath."

Great, that was just what I needed: a ghost who didn't want to talk. With that and a sheriff who didn't want to investigate, how in the world would this murder ever get solved?

7

W hile Willa talked to her ghosts, Pandora lazed
in her bed on the wide ledge of the large shop
window, trying to catch up on her catnap. She'd known
something was drastically wrong earlier and had tried to
warn the humans, but as usual, they'd buried their noses
in their coffees and ignored her. Oh well, they knew now.
And if her suspicions were true, she'd better take advantage of this quiet time to catch a few Z's.

She'd just about drifted off when a loud *thunk* jolted
her awake. She jerked her head up from the bed to see
Fluff leering at her through the glass. His human, Felicity, was nowhere to be found. Pandora hissed at him, and
he returned the sentiment.

"Your days are numbered, kitty," Fluff said to Pandora
through the glass. "My human is compiling the ingredi-

ents to reverse the pleasantry charm, and soon Mystic Notch will be a whole different town."

Despite the concern churning inside her, Pandora proceeded to groom her paws as if Fluff were nothing more than an annoying gnat. "Whatever. Where's Felicity? Does she know you're off-leash?"

Fluff puffed out his chest even farther. "Of course, she knows. My human's not tied to me. She trusts me. Even sent me off to investigate on my own. Not that you'd understand it. Our communication's much more developed than your pathetic attempts to control your human."

Pandora gave him a wilting glare. "My human can beat yours hands down. We aren't worried about you and your schemes. And I think you're bluffing about the ingredients. No one knows where they are, least of all Felicity."

Teeth bared, Fluff let out a menacing growl, and Pandora suppressed a smile of satisfaction.

Bingo! Baiting her nemesis had been easier than she'd anticipated. Judging by Fluff's response to her taunt, she'd been right. Felicity had no idea where the ingredients were. A bit of her tension eased.

"For your information," Fluff hissed, "my human has an ace up her sleeve, and you'll never guess what it is."

"Murder?" Pandora asked, blinking at him slyly.

"What? No." Fluff scowled. "What are you talking about?"

Pandora jerked her head toward Jack's Cards, down the street.

Her nemesis glanced over, looking confused. "That's not true. You're just trying to change the subject."

"Go see for yourself if you don't believe me."

"Fine. I will." Fluff started off down the sidewalk, his fluffy tail high in the air, then stopped and looked back at Pandora, saying, "You and your little gang of kitties are going down!"

Pandora wasn't worried. Well, not *overly* worried. She knew the cats of Mystic Notch could overpower Fluff. They'd done it before. But the fact that she now had evidence straight from the horse's mouth that Felicity was trying to get all the ingredients worried her. And nagging at her subconscious was Fluff's reaction to Jack's death. It was obvious that Fluff had been surprised, which meant that either Felicity wasn't involved in that, or she'd left Fluff at home when she'd done the deed. Felicity was still her main suspect for the break-ins, so that raised the question, why would she leave Fluff at home when she went to Jack's?

8

Striker came over that night, as promised, bringing Chinese food this time. Pandora lurked around the coffee table in the living room while we ate. She looked like she was listening to our conversation, but I was pretty sure she just wanted some pork fried rice.

"Any luck talking to you-know-who today?" Striker asked me around a mouthful of shrimp lo mien.

"Jack, you mean?" At his nod, I shook my head. "You know how persnickety they can be, especially the new ones. But I did have an interesting chat with Robert and Franklin. They said Jack's ghost has been hovering around, so at least there's that."

"Cool." Striker set aside his plate to pull out the notebook he carried around with him at work. "I took notes earlier when I talked to Gus about the investigation, and

I was able to dig up a bit of new information myself this afternoon."

He set the handwritten notes along with a few other papers on the coffee table then grabbed his plate again. Not to be left out, Pandora jumped up and laid atop the papers, knocking the extra napkins on the floor. I shooed her away so we could see the notes again.

"First off," Striker said, "Jack was killed with his own gun. The one he kept at the store. Gertie said the time of death was around ten p.m."

"Huh." I nibbled on an eggroll without really tasting it. "That is interesting. Go on."

"Mew!" Pandora jumped up again, batting at the notebook.

"Yes, we know you want to hear the details," Striker said to her as he gently lifted her off the table and placed her on the floor. She scowled at him, giving her tail a little flick, as if shaking off the indignity of being picked up and placed somewhere by a human.

"We also discovered the payroll was missing." Striker wiped his mouth then flipped a page in the notebook. "His wife said he brings it to the bank on Thursday mornings and usually has it all set in one of those big pleather bank deposit bags the night before."

"So, something *was* stolen this time." I set my plate aside. "That's the first time anything has gone missing with one of these break-ins."

"Yep." Striker finished his food then sat back against the cushions. "What we need to figure out is how the killer got Jack's gun. From what Gus said, there didn't appear to be a struggle at all. He was sitting down when he was shot."

"Merow!" Pandora jumped up again. At least this time she took care not to mess up the notes. She sat on the table, looking down at them as if she could read them.

"What about evidence from the previous break-ins? Anything to connect them?" I asked.

"Not much. All the locks were picked, so that's the same." He spread the papers out and pointed to one that had copies of pictures on it. "Here're some of the things in the evidence bags."

It wasn't much. A few pictures of scrapes on the metal and chips on the wood near the locks. Some snapshots of notes scribbled on the back of a coffee receipt in Gus's hand that were hard to decipher. A picture of a partial footprint from the curio store break-in, lots of photos of fingerprints, a bag with a few short whiteish-bleach-blond hairs from the lamp shop break-in, a picture of a shirt collar with something red smeared on it. I looked closer at that one. "What's this? Doesn't look like blood."

Striker nodded. "That's Jack's collar, and it looks like lipstick to me."

I gave him a raised brow look. "Hmmm... I wonder if it's Brenda's color."

"Me too," Striker said. He pointed to the crumpled notes on the back of the receipt. "At least Gus is investigating, though I can't make sense of her notes."

"I'm sure she is." I sank back into the couch. I did think Gus was investigating, just not with her usual zeal. Which meant I might need to lend a hand. After all, I had investigator instincts from my former job, and even though Gus and I did argue a lot, I didn't want to see her fail. Not to mention, a killer was running loose, and we needed to stop whoever it was before there was another victim.

The lipstick seemed the biggest clue. The footprint was too small of a section to narrow it down. The fingerprints wouldn't help, either, since half the population of Mystic Notch and tons of tourists were in the shops these days. "I still don't understand why our burglar suddenly resorted to murder."

"Me either." Striker yawned and stretched, giving me a nice view of his muscled torso. "Maybe Jack surprised him, and the crook got nervous and shot him. There was no evidence that the burglar wrestled the gun away from Jack, so we still aren't sure exactly how it happened."

"Man, this would be so much easier if we could talk to Jack's ghost," I said, snuggling into Striker's side as he put his arm around my shoulders, pulling me close.

Pandora was back on the coffee table, sniffing the notes along with our empty plates and batting at the paperweight. I couldn't shake the feeling that she was trying to tell me something. Last night when I'd looked into the paperweight, I hadn't seen anything, but maybe I should look again now. After all, the previous evening, I hadn't really had a specific focus, and now I did. Jack. I sat up and grabbed the heavy glass object and held it in my palm to stare into its crystal depths.

An image glimmered there, and I peered close, my pulse racing.

Was this the answer we'd been seeking?

Was it Jack trying to communicate with us from beyond the grave?

Squinting, I leaned close enough that my nose bumped against the cold glass, but all I saw inside was a martini glass with an olive and lipstick on the rim. Not helpful at all. Unless the spirits were trying to tell me to drink more.

Actually, a drink sounded pretty darned good right about then.

"I'm going to make a martini," I said, pushing to my feet. "Want one?"

"Huh?" Striker raised a dark brow at me then shrugged. "Sure, why not? I'm off duty."

We went to the kitchen and mixed up a batch. I had a few jars of olives, so we added some juice to make dirty martinis then took our glasses and the shaker back to the living room to sip. I was just pouring our second round when Jack's ghost appeared in the center of the room. I nearly dropped the shaker but managed to save it at the last second. I'd have to remember the alcohol trick the next time I needed to speak to the dead.

Jack seemed confused, as I'd expected. Striker looked from the ghost to me then nodded.

I approached the apparition slowly, not wanting to spook him. "Jack? Did you see who shot you?"

Jack looked around the kitchen, his ethereal gaze finally settling on me. "Shot? Is that what happened?"

"Yes. I'm sorry." I stopped a few feet away from him. "You didn't know?"

"No." Jack looked perplexed. "The last thing I remember is closing my eyes."

"Someone broke into your store, Jack," Striker said, moving to stand beside me. "Didn't that wake you up?"

The ghost shook his head. "I guess I was really tired."

He didn't seem particularly keen to have them find his killer, which was odd. Most ghosts I'd dealt with had that as their number-one priority. Not Jack, though. He seemed more interested in looking around my kitchen, then he moved into the living room, staring at all my grandmother's furniture and antiques.

"This looks like a place that would have some old baseball cards," Jack said. "Have you looked, Willa?

Sometimes they're hidden in drawers or books." He tried to take a book off the bookshelf, but his hand passed right through it.

Striker exhaled slowly, his expression frustrated. "So, you never saw who came into your shop?"

"Nope." Jack was still fixated on my books. "Like I said, I was sitting at the back of the store. I guess the burglar didn't know I was in the shop."

"Do you usually sleep with your gun?" Striker asked.

That got Jack's attention. He turned back toward us, his gaze narrowed. "Did I have it with me? I usually keep it in the drawer near the register."

"You don't remember that either?" I asked, doing my best to quell my irritation.

"No, not really," he said.

"How about we go over the timeline and see if that helps your memory?" I was desperate to get some kind of useful information out of this. "You said you were in your store like usual, and then you closed up for the night. But instead of leaving, you decided to sleep in the back?"

"Yes, that's right. I wanted to keep an eye on the store. Lots of valuable cards, and I didn't want the thief to get them."

Striker and I exchanged a glance. He asked, "When did you get in that day? Did any customers come in?"

Jack was now perusing the items on my desk. "I was there all day. There were lots of customers off and on."

"And you worked alone all day and were alone that night?" Striker asked.

"Does that matter?" Jack fired back, his tone a bit cagey. "Obviously I wasn't alone, because someone killed me." He tried to open a couple of the drawers but had no luck, being a ghost and all. "Listen, Willa. If you don't have any sports cards, I'm outta here."

"Yes, but don't you want—"

Jack didn't let me finish the sentence. He simply vanished, leaving me and Striker to stare at each other.

"Well, that wasn't helpful at all," I said, throwing my hands up in exasperation.

"No, it wasn't." Striker sat back down in his chair at the table and frowned into his empty martini glass. "Maybe he needs some time to get his memory back. It sounded like he didn't even know he'd been shot, and we kind of surprised him with that news. Hopefully, he'll remember more after he thinks about it."

"I hope you're right, because his memory of the events could be very helpful. He's the only one who knows what happened."

Striker's expression turned grim. "That's not entirely true. There is one other person who knows. The killer."

The next morning, I hurried from the town parking lot to the bookstore, resisting the urge to stop in front of Jack's Cards and study the crime scene. The yellow tape was still up, but of course the police had cleared everything. There was nothing left to see.

The regulars were waiting for me at the door. An air of excitement rippled through their group, and I knew they were eager to discuss the murder. Not that anyone was glad Jack had been murdered, but my senior-citizen friends always liked the challenge of tossing around ideas on solving crimes. I had to admit I was eager to talk to them. They often had interesting gossip that could help add insight to the cases.

I unlocked the door, and they hurried inside, Bing handing me a coffee as he passed. I tossed my bag on the counter, and we all congregated on the microsuede sofas and chairs again at the front of the store. Pandora was grooming herself in her bed by the windows as we discussed the murder.

"Did you get any inside information from Gus or Striker?" Josiah asked me.

"I didn't get much." I sipped my coffee. "But we already know there's a big difference now that someone has been murdered. And something was stolen too. Jack's bank deposit."

Hattie frowned. "Do you think they were after money this whole time, and the other shops didn't have any ready cash?"

Josiah leaned forward, his elbows on his knees. "Good question. I don't remember hearing that the thieves had taken cash, just that they hadn't taken any items."

"I'll ask Gus or Striker if there was cash in the registers at the other break-ins," I said.

"Such a shame that this one turned to murder," Bing said, shaking his head.

"And scary." Hattie sat forward. "Cordelia and I heard that the bank deposit was missing, during our hair appointments down at the Cut and Curl yesterday, and we've come to the conclusion that the only way someone could've known what time Jack made his bank deposits would be by casing the joint."

I bit back a smile at Hattie's old-time slang words.

"Which means that someone is watching." Cordelia glanced out the window and lowered her voice to a whisper. "They could be watching us right now."

"But if that's the case, then why break into the other stores? Wouldn't they have known the owner's deposit schedule and broken in when the till was full?" Josiah asked, frowning.

"Good point. I'm sure those other shop owners would have reported stolen money," I said. "Maybe the thief was mistaken about when they made their deposits, or they changed their routine. Perhaps we should talk to some of the other shop owners in the area. See if they saw anyone suspicious lurking around, that sort of thing."

"That might explain why the thief didn't realize Jack would be there. If he'd been watching the store, he would have figured Jack never stayed that late." Bing rubbed his chin. "Duane Crosby's ice cream shop is right next door. He'd have a clear view of Jack's place, and they share an entrance. He might have noticed someone hanging around."

"Yes, someone needs to ask the surrounding shop owners. That's what they always do on TV," Cordelia added, as if that confirmed it.

"Didn't Gus already do that?" Josiah asked.

"She did, but with how weird she's been acting lately, I can't guarantee she was all that thorough." I finished my coffee then stood. "Besides, it can't hurt to talk to a few of the shop owners ourselves."

"A Good Yarn is across the street from Jack's Cards. Maybe Mrs. Quimby noticed something," Cordelia suggested. "Plus, she was open late for the weekly knitting class the night Jack was killed. She might have seen the perpetrator."

"Perhaps," I said, my mind churning with the new information. The others began to file out of the shop, and I held the door for them, wishing them well as they passed me.

"Follow the money, I say," Hattie said on her way out, winking at me. "I bet whoever knew about the deposit is the killer."

* * *

HATTIE'S WORDS about following the money replayed in my head as I opened the store and restocked the shelves, then went into the back to make a desperate attempt to summon Jack's ghost again. I'd forgotten to ask him last night about the deposit—specifically, who knew about it. I wanted to ask now, but as usual, the ghost refused to play by my schedule.

I'd just given up when the bell over the door jangled, signaling a customer. I went back out front to find my sister leaning against the counter.

"Hey, sis," she said as I walked over to her. "I have a question."

My hopes soared, thinking maybe she was getting back on track with the investigation. I took it as a good sign. Maybe she was asking the shop owners if they'd seen anything, like I'd planned to do later.

"I was wondering if you had a nail file," Gus said.

Or not.

I sighed and pulled one out of the drawer beneath the counter to hand to her. She proceeded to walk over and plop down on the sofa and begin doing her nails. Desperate to get her mind back on work, I walked over and sat beside her.

"I have a question too," I said.

Gus grunted for me to continue as she inspected her nails.

"I was wondering if the shops that got broken into before had any cash money or if they'd changed their deposit schedule recently," I said.

She glanced up at me, her brows raised. "I can't imagine why you'd want to know that unless you knew that Jack's deposit was missing."

"Oh, umm…" I couldn't very well tell her that Striker had divulged that information or that we'd been discussing the case because we thought she wasn't doing a good job. Luckily the news had already been spread around town. "Hattie and Cordelia found out about it down at the hair salon, and it just made me wonder."

"Uh-huh. Well, for your information, no cash was lying around at the other stores. Proprietors didn't deposit regularly either."

Maybe Gus was paying more attention to this case than I'd thought. She certainly seemed to be on top of the bank-deposit angle. "So, have you checked to see who knew about Jack's payroll deposit?"

"Nope." Gus didn't even look at me, just frowned down at her fingers as she filed.

"How about checking if anyone had anything against Jack? A personal grudge maybe?"

Gus blew on her nails and scrubbed them on the front of her shirt then started on her second hand. "Nah."

Okay, maybe she wasn't paying attention to the case after all. I sighed and said a silent prayer for patience. "Have you gone back over the notes from the earlier robberies to find any common threads that could lead to a suspect?"

"Been busy. Haven't gotten around to it yet." Gus held her fingers out in front of her, admiring her work. "You know, now that you mention it, one of the store owners, Sarah Delaney, called into the station to say she saw someone near one of the break-in sites, but I never followed up because she's weird anyway. All those flowing black dresses and long fingernails. Probably can't be trusted."

"Sarah from the antiques shop?" My ears perked up. "Don't you think we should go talk to her, given what happened to Jack?"

Pandora got up and stretched, walking over to twine about my ankles as if she were interested in our conversation. I reached down and scratched behind her ears.

"I'm telling you, sis," Gus said, giving me an irritated stare. "Sarah's got nothing."

Then she reached down and began to pet Pandora herself. Highly unusual, to say the least. My stomach knotted tighter. Something was definitely off here, but I was determined to get to the bottom of all this strangeness. "Come on, Gus. We need to go talk to Sarah. What if another sheriff checks on your case? You don't want to get fired for slacking off." I stood and looked down at her. "Not to mention, there's a killer running around Mystic Notch."

Gus looked at me incredulously. "*What* other sheriff? Striker's the only one, and he thinks I'm handling this just fine."

Sure, he does.

I didn't want to override my sister's authority, but if I had to solve this case by myself, I would. Plus, Gus showing up at the antique store might make Sarah Delaney more forthcoming with her information.

"Get up, Gus," I said, grabbing my sister's arm. "Time to get to work."

Pandora meowed loudly, staring at Gus intently. So weird. Normally, my sister completely ignored the cat, but today she couldn't seem to stop petting her. When she started talking baby talk to her, I knew it was time to go. I tugged harder on her arm and finally got her to her feet, then nudged her toward the door.

"Time to get to Delaney's Antiques."

10

G us gave me little resistance, passively strolling down the street beside me, waving to shop owners as we passed. Delaney's Antiques was on a side street, a small shop packed to the brim with every kind of antique one could think of. Inside, it smelled of Lemon Pledge and sparkled with cut crystal vases and glasses that were displayed atop crochet doilies on every surface. Various pieces of polished mahogany and oak furniture were crammed into every available space, and colorful glassware, hand-painted plates, and jewelry gleamed from lighted glass cases.

Sarah was behind the register. She'd taken the shop over recently when her uncle had been arrested for murder. Sarah came from Salem, Massachusetts, and still dressed the part—all black clothes, long black hair, long dark nails. Typical witch attire.

She took one look at us, and her posture stiffened. I walked Gus over to the counter, not allowing her to get distracted by all the knickknacks in the shop, and kept my hand on her arm to hold her there.

"Hi, Sarah. I'm helping out Gus today with the investigation into what happened at Jack's place. She said you called the sheriff's office with information?" I tried to sound official, as if I was a member of the sheriff's office, as I nudged Gus in the ribs and gave her a pointed look.

"What?" Gus asked, frowning. My gaze darted between her and Sarah, and finally Gus said, "Yeah, I'm following up on your phone call."

"Well, I don't know anything about what happened to poor Jack," Sarah said, those long nails of hers tapping on the counter. "But I did see Felicity Bates skulking around the night the lamp shop got broken into."

"Well, shoot." Gus scoffed, waving her hand. "That's not helpful at all. Nothing was taken from the lamp shop. What about the night of the murder? Did you see her then?"

"No. I told you, I don't know anything about what happened to Jack," Sarah insisted.

"This doesn't get us anywhere." Gus pulled free from my grip and headed for a display of old plates. "I doubt Felicity's the killer."

My gut clenched tighter. Gus usually couldn't stand Felicity Bates and would have been all over this kind of information about her. My sister was definitely messed up.

"Besides," Gus said, picking up a plate and staring at the chicken painted on the front, "why would Felicity steal a bank deposit? She's rich." She put the plate down and crossed her arms, scowling at me. "Use your head, Willa. You can't just go off half-cocked and accuse people without evidence."

Now *that* was more like the old Gus. I felt encouraged. I was about to ask Sarah more questions when I was interrupted by her tiny Yorkie, Skeezits, bursting through the shop from where she'd been lying on an antique Chesterfield sofa in one of the alcoves. She tore toward one of the windows in the back, yapping as loudly as her little lungs would allow.

"What's the matter, baby?" Sarah asked, coming around the counter to follow the dog to the back of the store. "Is something out there?"

The dog had jumped up on top of an end table, still barking, to stare out a window.

"Wow," Sarah said, her eyes wide. "Look at that!"

I peered over her shoulder. Outside was a clowder of cats, one of them looking suspiciously like Pandora. Except that was impossible, considering I'd just locked her inside the bookstore.

* * *

Pandora stared out into the woods behind the antique store, remembering a night not so long ago when they'd had a showdown with Fluff. That night, the list of ingredients had been cast to the four winds, but what if some of it had come back? Were Fluff and Felicity really a threat? She peered between the trunks of the birches and maples into the darkest part of the woods as if there might be an answer back there, but all she got was the hoot of an owl and the rustling of squirrels in the leaves.

Pandora turned her attention back to the other cats who had gathered here. The cats had gotten a tip from one of the feral cats in town about someone digging behind Delaney's, so they had arranged to meet here. She'd used one of her usual escape routes in the closet of the bookstore right after Willa had dragged Gus out. With Willa gone, her absence wouldn't be noticed. Hopefully those nosy ghosts, Robert and Franklin, wouldn't tell.

Otis sniffed the air and shook his head. "My seventh sense is telling me one of the hidden ingredients is close by."

"Mine too," Sasha agreed, stretching her sleek Siamese body.

Inkspot narrowed his yellow gaze and scanned the location. "I, too, feel something, but I can't tell where it's buried. Anyone else?"

"Let me see if I can find it." Hope closed her eyes and

raised her Chimera face skyward. The young cat had been discovering more and more of her special abilities, and if she could locate one of the hidden ingredients, that would be a very good thing. Unfortunately, after a few moments, she hung her head and sighed. "Sorry, nothing. The magnetic energy in the earth is messing with my senses again."

"Well, I doubt there's anything here at the building," Pandora said, sitting back to groom her paws. "Most of the buildings in town weren't around when Hester Warren buried the ingredients. I'd say we'd be better served searching the forest and area around Mystic Notch. Most likely, she put the ingredients in the caves and perhaps a hollowed-out tree or two. Maybe even an old well."

"Did I mention that the feral cats I spoke with earlier also said they saw Felicity and Sarah Delaney digging around town?" Kelly chimed in.

"Together?" Pandora asked. She could have sworn the two of them did not get along.

Kelly's thick fluffy tail twitched as she spoke. "No. Separately."

"Might have mentioned that sooner." Otis gave her an annoyed glance, his tone dripping with sarcasm as usual. "It's no secret Sarah comes from Salem, and she's a witch."

"Plus, she and Felicity can't stand each other," Truffles chimed in.

"Hard to believe they'd be working together," Snowball added, shaking out her white fluffy fur. "They're enemies. Sparks fly whenever they run into each other."

"Just because they were both digging doesn't mean they are combining forces," Kelly said. "As I've already mentioned, my sources did see them at separate times."

"Let's hope they are not in cahoots." Inkspot seemed to consider that a moment. "Usually they stay out of the other's vicinity. If they ever team up, the consequences could be disastrous."

"I doubt they have." Pandora licked her paw and ran it behind her ear. "Curious thing, though, I don't believe Fluff had anything to do with the recent death at Jack's Cards."

"Oh?" Inkspot's whiskers twitched, his eyes getting rounder.

Otis huffed at her and pretended he wasn't interested in what she had to say even if Pandora herself thought it was interesting news.

"Yes, I spoke with him earlier, and he appeared to be quite surprised that someone had died." Pandora couldn't resist shooting a glance of superiority at Otis.

"Conspiring with the enemy?" Otis asked.

"No. I was in my cat bed in the bookstore window, and he came up to the glass. I took the opportunity to interrogate him." Pandora jerked her kinked tail high in the air.

"That's odd. Do you think that means Felicity is not behind all of these disturbances?" Sasha asked.

"Maybe Sarah Delaney was the one who killed Jack," Snowball said. "We know both she and Felicity are up to something but not necessarily together."

"Or if they are together, Sarah might have gone behind Felicity's back," Kelly suggested.

"Perhaps Felicity went behind Fluff's back and didn't bring him to Jack's Cards," Snowball suggested.

Otis scrunched his face. "Or Fluff was lying. He and Felicity are always together. Then again, she does keep him on a leash. Maybe she got sick of dragging him around and went out alone that night."

"With all the weird things going on around here, I wouldn't be surprised." Hope preened an errant whisker.

"I've confirmed that there is something weird going on with Gus," Pandora said. "I sniffed her when she was in the bookshop earlier, and she did not smell normal. Read her aura too. Everything's off. My human says she's not investigating her cases properly either."

"I feared that was the case," Inkspot said. "Without Gus, the humans of Mystic Notch will need our help more than ever."

"What did she smell like?" Hope asked, tilting her

head slightly so the black half of her face was closer to Pandora. "Certain scents mean different things."

Pandora wrinkled her nose then frowned. "It was almost like maple glazed doughnuts."

"Oh dear," Hope said, straightening. "She's been hexed."

The other cats gasped.

"Finally, something we can work with," Otis said, harrumphing. "Perhaps the killer hexed her so she won't investigate."

"Of course that's why." Pandora gave Otis a pointed glare. "Whoever is behind this wants free rein to do as they please."

"And now we know that the origins are magical," Hope said.

"Which narrows down our suspect list considerably." Otis cast a pointed look at the antique shop.

"If Gus has been hexed, we need to remedy that. We'll need to get an antidote potion from Elspeth," Inkspot said, his deep Morgan Freeman-esque voice booming off the brick wall behind them. "And we still need to figure out the connection between reversing the pleasantry charm, these break-ins, and Jack's death. There must be one."

Before any of the other cats could say more, a high-pitched yipping came from inside the antique store, and everyone jumped.

Pandora jerked her head in the direction of the yipping to see Willa peering out the window. Oops. Not good. Willa thought she was locked back inside the bookstore, and she didn't want her human to know she could get out anytime she wanted. Knowing Willa, she would search the place until she found Pandora's escape route. Willa only wanted to keep her safe, but Pandora needed her freedom. Besides, she could take care of herself. She was not the usual cat, without means of defending herself in times of danger.

"Sorry, guys. Gotta go!" Pandora said, taking off before Willa found her way out of Delaney's Antiques and discovered the gray cat really was hers.

11

I parted ways with Gus after leaving Delaney's Antiques and headed back toward the bookstore, wondering about the gray cat I'd seen. Of course it wasn't Pandora. How could she get out?

Surely there was more than one gray cat in Mystic Notch. In fact, there was quite a large population of feral cats that I sometimes helped care for. That was most likely them hanging around behind the store. Some of them did look like Elspeth's cats, but for all I knew, they all hung around together. Just because one was gray didn't mean it was Pandora.

My thoughts would be better spent thinking about Sarah Delaney. She'd seemed evasive, and I had to wonder if she was up to something. She also seemed like she was ready to point the finger at Felicity. Clearly she didn't like the other woman, though I couldn't say I blamed her there.

As I walked down the short side street, I passed A Good Yarn. Since it was across the street from Jack's Cards, Mrs. Quimby might have seen something that night, as she'd been there late due to her knitting class. Now seemed like as good a time as any to ask.

Inside, the shelves were brimming with a rainbow assortment of yarns. Mrs. Quimby had owned the store for decades and apparently hadn't seen fit to update it in that time either. Some of the advertisements for various yarns on the walls and papers tacked to the window were yellowed and the edges tattered, as if they were from the 1970s. A few of the patterns looked to be from that era too. I mean, who would knit a jumpsuit in this day and age?

Mrs. Quimby was behind the counter, her white hair smoothed back into a bun near the nape of her neck and the chain from her glasses glinting in the sunshine streaming through the front windows. She looked up at the sound of the bells on the door, smiling at me, though worry lurked in her gray eyes. "Willa, dear. How are you? Did you hear about what happened to poor Jack? Horrible thing. Just horrible. But I have faith in our local law enforcement. They'll find the responsible party, and all will be right again."

I wished I had the same confidence at the moment,

given how odd my sister was acting, but I didn't want to let Mrs. Quimby know that. No sense in worrying the kindly old lady. I smiled and walked up to the counter. "That's actually why I'm here, Mrs. Q. I wondered if I could ask you a few questions about what you remember from the night Jack died."

"Oh, of course, dear. Though I'm not sure how helpful I'll be. I was busy with a knitting class that night." Mrs. Quimby set aside the basket of things she'd been sorting through and focused her attention on me. "Ask away."

"Okay." Resting my hip against the counter, I concentrated on what Sarah had told me earlier and hoped to fill in some of the missing pieces. "What time did your knitting class end that night?"

"Nine."

So, about an hour prior to Jack's time of death, according to what Striker had told me from the ME's report. "Did you see anyone unusual lurking around the area?"

"Not anyone *unusual*," Mrs. Quimby said, frowning. "Just Duane and Jack, but that's not out of the ordinary since their shops are located over there."

"What about Felicity Bates?"

Mrs. Quimby scrunched her nose in distaste, and I bit back a smile. Clearly the woman was a good judge of character. "No, I didn't see her that night. Though I did catch her skulking around behind the lamp shop last week after dark."

"What were you doing behind the lamp shop?" I asked, confused.

"It's a free country, isn't it?" Mrs. Quimby said, uncharacteristically upset before she collected herself again. "I'm sorry, dear. It's just hard getting old. Honestly, I forgot where I parked my car and was looking for it." At my concerned stare, she waved me off. "I'm fine, dear. Really. Don't worry about me. I'm not going senile or anything."

"Of course not." I patted her arm, noticing the flyer for the knitting class on the counter. Class started at seven and got out at nine. Apparently they had tackled a knitted-socks project. "Do you keep a list of who comes to the class?"

"I don't need a list, dear. It's usually the same folks. Though not everyone comes each week."

"Do you remember who came to the class the night of the murder?" Even though Mrs. Quimby apparently hadn't seen anything fishy, maybe one of the other knitters had.

"Of course I do. There was Eloise Flaherty, Molly Saunders, Betty Wilder..." Mrs. Quimby's voice drifted off, and she squinted, as if trying to remember. "Anne Crosby might have been there. She comes sometimes. Oh, and poor Brenda McDougall. She insisted on following me home. No wait, that wasn't the night I forgot where my car was. That was last week."

"Are you sure?" I asked. My confidence in getting a list of potential witnesses faded.

"Of course I am." She glanced at a row of hooks on the wall, where I could see her car keys hanging. "It's so hard to find parking here in town sometimes. I have to park in one of the lots, and then I can't quite remember which one. Anyway, if you are asking because you think one of them might have seen something, you're barking up the wrong tree. The class gets out promptly at nine, and everyone hightails it out of here by quarter past. I heard Jack was killed around ten."

Mrs. Quimby's hands shook, and I realized I was being insensitive. Here she was, an old lady with a failing memory, and I was interrogating her like I was Jessica Fletcher. Clearly having someone murdered across the street would be disturbing.

"I'm sorry. I hope this isn't upsetting to you."

"Oh, no worries. I feel bad for Jack and Brenda, of course. But don't worry about me. I can take care of myself." She bustled over to one of the tall shelves that held skeins of yarn and started filling a basket. "I'm sorry I didn't see anything pertinent, but I'll let you know if I remember something. I'm not quite as senile as everyone thinks."

I watched her a moment then sighed, looking down

at the knitting-class flyer. Should I even bother asking the others that had been in the knitting class? For all I knew, the list she'd given me was wrong. Had she really seen Felicity behind the lamp shop? That might be something to mention to Striker, but exactly how bad *was* Mrs. Quimby's memory?

When I glanced back up at Mrs. Q, she'd turned from the display, her basket full, and was smiling at me. "Now what kind of yarn did you say you wanted today, dear?"

12

Back at the bookstore, I let myself in then glanced over to find Pandora snoozing away in her cat bed, just like I'd left her. Of course she was. Why I'd doubted it was beyond me, but here was the proof. That cat behind Delaney's hadn't been her.

I walked into the back of the store and started to open the new boxes of books that had arrived the prior day. Pandora must have woken because I could hear her at her food bowl. I was glad when she joined me in the stockroom. I could use her as a sounding board as I talked out the case. I knew she couldn't understand me, but I appreciated her meows, which seemed to come at all the appropriate times anyway.

"Do you know where I went earlier?" I asked the cat as I gathered a stack of books to carry out to the shelves in front. "I went and talked to Sarah Delaney at the antique store."

"Meow." The tone of her meow held disdain, reflecting my feelings about Sarah exactly.

"Yep. And she said she saw Felicity around the lamp store around the time it was broken into."

Pandora meowed again, as if this was no surprise to her.

I slid two books onto the shelf and moved down a row. "But then I stopped at Mrs. Quimby's on my way back here, and while she did see Felicity lurking around behind the lamp shop, she was kind of vague on when that was, and she didn't see Felicity the night of the break-in and murder at Jack's Cards." I sighed and bent to stick the last book in my pile onto the bottom shelf. "But she did mention seeing Duane and Jack."

Pandora gave a loud, prolonged meow at that information.

Straightening, I looked over at my cat and smiled as a new idea formed. "You're right. I should go talk to Duane next. If he was there that night, then he might've seen something, especially since he shared an entrance with Jack. Good thing I thought of that."

Pandora eyed me skeptically.

I was about to head back into the storeroom for more new books when the bells above the entrance jangled, and a woman walked in. I recognized her as the bartender from the Blue Moon.

"Hi," she said, tucking a piece of her short brunette hair behind her ear. The sunshine outside highlighted her blond streaks. "Your sister, Gus, referred me to you. Said you might have a copy of an out-of-print antique cocktail book I've been looking for. If not, she said you might be able to order it for me."

"Well, let's see what I can do," I said, leading her over to the counter.

"Thanks. I really appreciate it," she said. "Gus says you're a genius at finding old books."

My heart swelled a bit with pride at my sister's rare compliment. Gus usually never said such nice things about me. It made me more determined than ever to help her solve Jack's murder so she kept her job and her reputation intact. Hopefully, once all this was over, Gus would go back to normal and do her work properly again, but if her new habit of being semi-nice to me remained, I supposed that wouldn't be a problem.

I went behind the counter and woke up my computer then signed into the search database I used. "Do you have the title of the book you're looking for?"

"I do." She rattled it off, and I typed it in, hit Enter, and a few moments later, got a hit.

Squinting at the screen, I smiled. "Looks like you're in luck. They have a copy in an old bookstore in California for only twelve bucks, including shipping. I can order it for you and let you know when it comes in. Shouldn't be more than a few days. Sound good?"

"Sounds great," she said, handing me the money. "Thanks so much again, Ms. Chance."

"You're welcome. And please," I said, handing her back a receipt. "Call me Willa."

13

The bookshop was unusually busy that afternoon, and I never got time to go over to Duane's ice cream shop. When I locked up at five, the line for ice cream was twenty deep. He would be too busy to talk, so I headed home to meet Striker. Luckily he'd brought dinner, and we compared notes over Thai food.

"I stopped by the sheriff's office on my way here, and it didn't look like Gus had uncovered any more clues. There was no DNA found at the scene and hundreds of partial prints, which is understandable, given it's a store," Striker said around a mouthful of pad khing sod. "We found those hairs at the lamp shop after the break-in but nothing like that at Jack's. Still, Gus is running those hairs through analysis at the crime lab, just in case. Not sure if she has a rush on it or anything, though."

"Given her relaxed attitude toward things, I doubt

that." I swallowed a bite of my pad see ew, the sweet soy sauce and wok-fried noodles the perfect complement to the crispy broccoli. Major yum. "Sounds like things are stalled."

"For now." Striker wiped his mouth then took a swig of his soda. "How about you? Discover anything interesting?"

"I did." I smiled. "I went over and talked to Sarah Delaney at the antique store, then stopped by Mrs. Quimby's on my way back to the bookshop."

"And?" He raised a dark brow at me.

"And Sarah told me she saw Felicity Bates behind the lamp shop the night it was broken into, and Mrs. Quimby also saw Felicity behind that shop." I frowned, remembering Mrs. Quimby's memory issues. "Though I'm not so sure we can count on her for the exact timing. I am sure that she did see Felicity back there, though."

"Interesting." Striker paused and blinked at me. "Assuming the break-ins were all by the same person, that does make Felicity seem suspicious. But why would she want to kill Jack?"

"Good question."

"Meow!" Pandora seemed to agree. Either that or she wanted Striker to feed her another piece of shrimp from the carton of shrimp lo mein.

Striker sat back and pushed the rest of his food aside, exhaling slow. "So, basically we're back where we started, then. Man, if only we had some security footage or something from that night to see who was going in and out of Jack's store."

"Mrs. Quimby said she didn't see anyone suspicious lurking around. Just people who would normally be there—Duane and Jack. She did have a knitting class that night, and I got the names of some of the attendees." I took the piece of paper on which I'd written the names after my visit to Mrs. Quimby out of my back pocket and handed it to Striker. "Not sure how reliable that list is, and besides, she said they all left by nine fifteen."

Striker looked at the list. "It's worth asking them. Maybe someone saw something unusual before they left. Jack's time of death was ten p.m., but the killer was probably on the premises before that."

"I think we should try to summon Jack again," I said, clearing away our plates while Striker put the leftovers in the fridge. "He might be more forthcoming with information. We can ask him if he knows Felicity and who would know about the bank deposits."

"That's a good idea." Striker leaned in to kiss my cheek then walked over to the liquor cabinet. "Martinis again?"

"You know it," I said, laughing as I rinsed off the dishes and stuck them in the dishwasher. Once we were settled in the living room, on the sofa, drinks in hand, I glanced at the paperweight again, but I didn't see anything unusual. Odd, though, as it seemed I was drawn to the shiny bauble. Pandora, too, if the way she kept batting at it was any indication. Finally I gave up thinking the paperweight might enlighten me and sat back on the sofa.

It took about half a pitcher of martinis before Jack finally made an appearance, and neither Striker nor I were feeling any pain.

Setting my empty glass on the coffee table, I leaned forward to rest my elbows on my knees and fixed ghostly Jack with a pointed stare. He was back to snooping through my things again, same as the night before.

"Who knew about your nightly deposits, Jack? Someone from the bank? A neighboring store owner? Maybe someone from across the street?"

He gave me an irritated glance then went back to his rummaging. "No idea. I always made the deposit on Thursday morning. Everyone at the bank would know that and most anybody nearby my shop."

Including Mrs. Quimby, I thought before I brushed the idea aside. She was a sweet old lady. No way she could be behind the break-ins or Jack's death.

"Why do you keep asking me about that night anyway?" Jack fussed, scowling at me. "I don't care if they catch the person or not. What I want to know is if you found any old sports cards." I shook my head, and he sighed. "Well, if you do, then let me know. I'll give you a good valuation on them."

"Hey, Jack," Striker said. "How well do you know Felicity Bates?"

Jack jerked his head up from the credenza he was looking in. "That crazy lady who thinks she's a witch and walks her cat on a leash?"

"Yep."

"I don't know her. She came in once for tarot cards, and I sent her on her way. Don't have time for frou-frous like that," Jack said.

"When did she come in?" Striker asked. "Was it the night you were killed?"

"Nope. Few weeks ago."

"And you didn't see her around that night?" I asked. I had to admit I was hoping to tie Felicity into all of this. Plus I was sure she'd killed someone once before, so she probably wouldn't bat an eyelash at doing it again.

"No." Jack looked bored with the line of questioning, and his ghostly presence started to fade.

Striker hastily added, "I know you don't want to think about it anymore, but if you could remember anything at all about your killer, that would be—"

"I don't, okay?" Jack said testily. "And whatever happened, it had nothing to do with what I was doing before I was killed, all right? Now drop it. I need to go. It's happy hour on the spirit side, and the booze flows freely. See you."

He vanished in a puff of irritated mist. I exhaled and sat back, holding out my glass for a refill. "That is so strange. Usually the ghosts pester me to find their killer so they can move on to whatever comes next, but Jack doesn't seem to care so much. In fact, it seems like he wants the opposite."

"Agreed." Striker kissed the top of my head then sipped his drink, pulling me closer. "Jack is acting weird. And if you ask me, something doesn't add up."

14

"If you ask me, something doesn't add up," Inkspot said.

The cats were meeting in Elspeth's barn to talk about the strange goings-on in Mystic Notch. Pandora had had no problem sneaking out. Turned out this new martini ghost-rousing routine made Willa and Striker less observant of what she was doing. She could have opened the front door and walked out of the house right in front of them, and they might not have noticed. Silly humans.

Despite the disturbing events going on in town, Pandora was not afraid to walk the path through the woods alone. She'd been doing it for a long time and could traverse the path with her eyes closed. Even if somehow she veered from the path, she could navigate by the moon and stars. She was afraid of nothing in the woods—the night owls, tall oaks, and other forest creatures were her friends. But underneath her brave exterior, a deep dark fear did lurk. Would the woods and its creatures still be so friendly if the pleasantry spell was reversed?

No sense in worrying too much about that. The cats had never failed to save the day before, and this time would be no different. Pandora stretched and snuggled farther down into the hay in Elspeth's barn as the November wind howled outside. The hay, though not as comfortable as her plush cat bed, was warm, and she loved the earthy scent. It reminded her of horses and spring days, a welcome image, considering winter was soon to come.

"I tell you, Felicity Bates is behind this." Otis raised his nose in the air. "Her and that devil cat, Fluff."

Sasha blinked slowly at him. "But we haven't found any evidence that she was in Jack's card store."

"Maybe not," Kelly piped in, giving her big, floofy Maine coon tail a twitch. "But she had been digging around town. That much we do know."

"And don't forget Sarah Delaney," Hope added. "She's been digging around too."

"She is just as disagreeable as the Bates woman," Sasha said.

"And that vile dog!" Otis hissed. "Scuzzball or whatever its name is."

"Scuse-its," Snowball said.

Kelly jumped down from the loft. "No, it's Squeakems, I think."

"Skeezits," Pandora said. "But why would either of them kill Jack? Willa has been talking to his ghost, and he seems quite evasive."

"Really?" Inkspot glanced at her out of the corners of his eyes. "I wonder if more is going on here than meets the eye."

"Maybe Jack was in on the break-ins," Snowball suggested.

"He denies knowing Felicity," Pandora said. "But I think he's not telling the whole truth."

"I think a lot of the people involved are not telling the whole truth," Inkspot said. "We must remain vigilant. The person behind this could be anyone, and we don't want to get caught up in only looking at Felicity and Sarah. Remember the other times when the perpetrator was that who we least suspected?"

The others nodded at Inkspot's stern warning.

"There are many in town who hide their true desire to see the dark side take over behind a façade," Hope said. "We'd do best not to forget that."

"Agreed." Pandora fixed each of her feline comrades with a pointed stare. "But there is something else I find most troubling at the moment. Gus. She's the sheriff in this town. We need to get her back to her former crime-solving self before it's too late. My human is trying to fill in for her, but she could get hurt. She's tracking a killer and doesn't even have a gun the way Gus does!"

"I was able to communicate to Elspeth that Gus had been hexed," Tigger offered, soothing Pandora's frazzled nerves a bit. "She said it sounded like a potion hex, and she was going to make an antidote potion to reverse it. But how we'll get Gus to drink it is another matter entirely."

"That's the human's problem." Otis sniffed imperiously.

"It's too bad we can't figure out who hexed Gus," Inkspot said. "Because it's clear that person does not want Gus investigating. And *that* would seem to indicate the person who hexed her is likely the one who has been breaking in everywhere and has recently turned into a killer."

15

The next morning, I awoke with a headache. Whether it was from tossing and turning over the strange way Jack's ghost had acted and my ominous feelings about his murder or the martinis I'd consumed in order to conjure him, I wasn't sure. A few aspirins took care of it, and Pandora and I arrived only ten minutes later than usual to open the shop.

The regulars were all there, wearing thick fall sweaters and shuffling their feet. Relief spread over their faces when they saw me coming.

"Late start today, Willa?" Hattie asked as I unlocked the door.

Cordelia leaned in to her sister and faux-whispered, "Maybe that nice Eddie Striker made her late."

I ignored her and hid the blush creeping into my cheeks by opening the door and ushering them in.

"We were a little worried, Willa, what with everything going on." Bing handed me the Styrofoam coffee cup, and we all sat down on the sofa and chairs.

"Sorry. I woke up a little under the weather." I peeled back the plastic lid of the coffee cup and inhaled the earthy scent. Heaven. I took a tentative sip. It wasn't too hot, so I took a bigger sip, willing the caffeine into my system so it could do its job.

"Worried about Jack's murder?" Hattie glanced in the direction of Jack's shop.

"Mew." Pandora trotted around the group. Her kinked tail bobbed in the air as she rubbed against their ankles and headbutted their hands to remind them to scratch behind her ears.

"Sort of." I took another sip.

"I hope you're not worried about Gus." Josiah leaned forward in his chair, his concerned eyes meeting mine. "I've noticed she isn't acting quite herself."

"Well, now that you mention it, I have been a bit worried." Pandora stopped in front of me and rubbed against my leg. I petted the top of her head, the soft, silky fur giving me comfort. "But she's probably just having an off day, or maybe she isn't feeling well. I mean, I'm sure she has things with the investigation under control." The last thing I wanted was for my regulars to worry about Gus not having a handle on catching the killer who could be running amok in Mystic Notch.

Hattie reached over and patted my knee. "Don't worry, dear. Even if Gus is moving slowly on things, the killer will be caught. Especially with Jack's wife looking into things now."

I stopped mid-sip and frowned at her over the rim of my cup. "Jack's wife is looking into things? How do you know that?"

"Oh, Myra, down at the Cut and Curl, saw her going through the trash out in the alley," Cordelia answered for her twin. "Myra's back door opens to the same alleyway as Jack's card store."

"What was she doing in the trash?" I made a mental note to ask Striker if they'd looked through the trash for clues. Of course they had. I mean, that was investigating 101, wasn't it?

Cordelia shrugged. "I'm not sure. Myra asked Brenda what she was doing, and she got all tearful and said if the police weren't going to do anything about Jack's death, then she sure was."

"Jeez, that's kind of premature to assume the police aren't going to do anything," Josiah said. "Looked like they did a thorough job at the card store to me."

"Well, you know how grieving widows are," Hattie said. "They want answers right away. But we know it takes time to investigate these things."

"It's only been a few days. I'm sure something will break." Bing stood and started toward the door. "I'm gonna get back home. Brushing up on my card tricks today."

"Yep, gotta get to the post office." Josiah followed him to the door.

"And we need to go shopping. There's a sale at the Creekside Dress Shop." Cordelia pulled Hattie off the couch. As they approached the door, Cordelia turned back to me. "Don't worry, dear. I'm sure Gus will come around."

I remained on the purple sofa for a moment, taking that new information in. Was Gus's apparent lack of enthusiasm so noticeable that the citizens were starting to investigate now? I'd better help her up her game before something else happened.

The door opened, and Pepper came in. Seeing me on the sofa, she wrinkled her forehead in concern and came and sat beside me. "Hey, Willa. How are things going? You look a bit tired today."

"Probably because I am." I sighed and set my empty cup on the table before us. "It's exhausting trying to do the work of two people. Until Gus is back to her old self and doing her job again, I feel like I have two jobs."

"I'm sorry." Pepper rubbed my back. "Would it help to talk the case out?"

"Maybe." I sat back and closed my eyes, focusing on what I knew so far. "We don't have a lot to go on, frankly.

First, a string of prior break-ins where nothing was stolen."

"Which means they weren't looking to rob the place," Pepper said. "They were looking for something instead."

"Right." I opened my eyes and straightened. "Did they find it at Jack's? Is that why they killed him?"

"What about the deposit?" Pepper asked. "You told me it was stolen from his store."

"I'm not sure about that." I shook my head. "The other stores didn't have any cash lying around, it's true, but there were other valuables. Wouldn't they have taken those and sold them for cash if that was what they were after?"

"Probably. *If* they were after money." Pepper pursed her lips, narrowing her gaze.

"You're thinking about that list again, aren't you?"

"Well, if no money was taken..." She let her voice trail off.

"That doesn't make any sense either, though. If the thieves were looking for these ingredients, then why take the money from Jack's?"

"You said yourself the other shops didn't have any money. Maybe the thieves didn't take valuable items because they knew the sale of those items might be traced back to them, but when they saw cash lying around, they grabbed it."

"That takes Felicity Bates out, then. She's not that

smart." Even Pandora agreed with that, judging by the little meow that came from her cat bed in the window.

"But if this is about the ingredients, then that negates the theory that the person knew Jack's routine and broke in on purpose because they knew the deposit money would be there," Pepper said.

"Good point. So we're back to square one."

Pepper nodded and sank back into her chair. "Were you able to summon Jack's ghost and talk to him about what happened?"

"Yep. Twice. But he's acting a little weird too. Like he could care less whether his murder is solved or not." I exhaled slowly. "So strange. Last night when I talked to him, he was evasive and cagey about what he was doing that night. I think he might be embarrassed that he can't remember, but he shouldn't be. New ghost amnesia is quite common."

"Hmm." Pepper tapped a finger against her lips. "You said before that there was lipstick on his collar when they examined the body at the shop."

"Yep."

"I wonder if that has something to do with why he's acting weird." She gave me a side-glance. "Maybe he had another woman in his life besides Brenda."

"Maybe he did. Striker and I did discuss that briefly. That would sure explain his odd behavior." Feeling a renewed sense of energy, I pushed to my feet. "I need to find out if Brenda wears bright-red lipstick."

"I can help you there," Pepper said, pushing to her feet beside me. "What better way to get a sample than to bring the grieving widow some tea and scones from my shop to give our condolences?"

16

An hour later, Pepper and I were knocking on the door to Brenda's house. I had a bag of freshly baked chocolate chip scones in my hands while Pepper carried the quilted tote with all her tea supplies. She'd made a special batch of relaxation blend just for Brenda, hoping it might make the woman want to open up and share with us.

Our plan was to get Brenda to drink some of the tea to calm her, then I would excuse myself to use the bathroom and search for the lipstick. We didn't want to ask her outright about it, because we didn't want to upset her, just in case the lipstick wasn't hers.

I raised my hand to knock a second time when the door suddenly opened.

Brenda looked surprised, her brown curls in disarray

around her head. "Willa. Pepper. What are you doing here?"

"We thought we'd stop by and see how you're doing," Pepper said, giving the woman a kindly smile. "We brought tea and scones and thought we might have a nice visit."

"Oh." Brenda's gaze darted from the tray in Pepper's hands to the bag in mine. "Well, I guess that's fine. Come in."

We walked into her quaint two-story Cape Cod home, and the first thing I noticed was the abundance of knickknacks. Everything from figurines to spoons. Probably an occupational hazard, given the nature of Jack's business. Even though he dealt in sports cards, I knew that it was hard to go to the auctions where cards were bought and not buy some of the other items. I'd done the same myself while waiting for a book lot to come up to the auction block.

We took a seat in the living room, before the crackling fire, and Brenda brought out plates and napkins for the scones while Pepper set everything out. Then we settled in for our conversation.

"How are you doing?" I asked, doing my best to convey my concern through my tone. "It must be hard, what you're going through."

"It is," Brenda said, her hand shaking slightly as she sipped her tea. Gradually, the lines of stress on her face eased, though, and her stiff posture sagged. Score one for the relaxation tea. I glanced sideways at Pepper, and she smiled. Brenda sighed. "I'm still so upset about Jack's death. I'm not eating. I'm not sleeping. It's awful. Just awful."

"I'm sure it is. I can't imagine what you've been going through." Pepper reached over and placed her hand atop Brenda's in her lap. "But that's why we're here. Anything you need to talk about, feel free."

"I'm sorry," I said, setting my tea aside. "But may I use your restroom?"

"Sure." Brenda pointed down a nearby hall. "Second door on your right."

"Thank you." While they continued talking, I went to investigate. Once inside the bathroom, I locked the door behind me then turned on the faucet so Brenda wouldn't hear me snooping. I checked the cabinets and the drawers for red lipstick but only found clear lip gloss. Darn. I flushed the toilet and washed my hands. Maybe she kept the lipstick in her bedroom? I glanced in but didn't see any cosmetics on the bureau and couldn't risk her catching me snooping through her drawers, so I went back to the living room.

Brenda wasn't wearing any lipstick at all today, and she seemed more than suitably upset about losing her husband. My gut said she wasn't Jack's killer. I took my seat again and picked up my tea, giving a subtle shake of my head to let Pepper know I'd come up empty in my search. "I hope you don't mind me asking, Brenda, but who else do you think might've known about the bank deposits?"

Pepper nibbled on a scone, her gaze intent on Brenda. "Sarah Delaney, maybe? Or what about Felicity Bates?"

"No. Neither of them, that I'm aware of. We never really knew either of them well." Brenda finished her tea then picked up a scone. "This is all delicious. Thanks for thinking of me."

"No problem," I said.

"My husband was just trying to protect his shop." Brenda wiped her mouth with a napkin. "He was hoping to catch the burglar himself so no one in town had to worry anymore."

"Really?" Pepper frowned over at me before looking back at Brenda. "So, Jack was setting a trap for someone?"

"No. Not a trap," she said around another bite of scone. "He was just protecting his collectibles. I mean, we have insurance and all, but if items get stolen, we only get replacement cost, not the profit we'd make on the sale. He was keeping watch to make sure no one got in…"

Her voice drifted off, and she gazed out the window, almost as if in a daze, before speaking again. "You know,

now that I think about it, there might've been one person who knew about Jack's deposits. Duane Crosby. Being neighbors, they sometimes went to the bank for each other."

I nodded. This confirmed the information I'd gotten the day before. Mrs. Quimby had mentioned seeing Duane, which wasn't unusual, considering the stores shared an entrance, but what if Duane really was the culprit?

"But then again, no matter how much I pestered him to change up his schedule, Jack always went to the bank on Thursday mornings, like clockwork. Having a routine like that would make it easy for anyone who was the least bit observant to track his banking habits. I tried to warn him. I did."

She started to dissolve into tears, and Pepper handed Brenda a fresh napkin to dry her eyes.

While she sniffled, I tried a different question. "Someone mentioned seeing you out in the alleyway behind Jack's shop, going through the trash the other day. You aren't thinking of investigating yourself, are you?"

"What?" Brenda looked up at me, her eyes red. "No. Of course not. I have confidence in the police. I just would like to know who killed my husband. But I wouldn't be averse to things moving a bit faster. Pardon me, Willa. I know the sheriff is your sister, but she doesn't seem all that interested in bringing in a suspect on my husband's case. And I need closure."

My gut churned, and I made sympathetic noises. "I'm sure the police looked there already. Did you find anything they might have overlooked?"

"No. Nothing." More tears fell. "My poor, poor Jack."

Pepper patted Brenda's hand as Brenda sobbed into one of the embroidered linen napkins Pepper had brought. I glanced down, saw a knitting bag at Brenda's feet, and remembered Mrs. Quimby's knitting class that night. I wasn't sure if Striker and Gus had asked any of the attendees if they'd seen anything. Might as well ask Brenda while she was under the relaxing effects of the special tea.

"I see you have a knitting project going. Is that from Mrs. Quimby's knitting class?"

Brenda glanced down at the bag and nodded. She blew her nose on the linen napkin. Pepper made a face, no doubt making a mental note to make sure that napkin got special laundering.

Brenda picked the project out of the bag and held it up. It was still attached to the needles, but I could see it was a sock done in pink-and-orange yarn. "I was knitting it for Jack."

"It's very nice. Did you spend the whole class on that?" I asked.

"Yes. We all did. We do the same project each time."

Brenda admired her handiwork, a slight smile coming to her face, then the smile faded, and her eyes turned weepy. "Maybe if I hadn't been working on this so hard, Jack would still be alive."

"How so?" Pepper asked.

Brenda put the sock back in the bag carefully so as not to drop a stitch. "The class had let out at nine o'clock as usual, but I was in the middle of a row and wanted to get it done. The other ladies took off pretty quick. I knew Jack was staying at the store, and I was going to pop over and visit him."

My hopes rose. Maybe she'd seen something. I waited for her to continue, but she just stared at the coffee table, so I prompted her. "And what happened when you went over? Did you see someone?"

"No, that's the thing. I never went over."

"Why not?" Pepper asked.

"Mrs. Quimby had misplaced her car." Brenda shook her head. "It's not the first time she's done that, and we're all a bit worried about her. Anyway, I drove her around town, looking for the car. I didn't want her walking around alone, what with the break-ins and all..."

"That's nice of you," Pepper said. "Then you never went to visit Jack?"

Brenda shook her head. "No. It took us a while to find Mrs. Quimby's car, and then I was worried she might not find her way home, so I followed her. I'd texted Jack to let him know when we got out of class, and he said he was turning in, so maybe I should go straight home. After I saw Mrs. Quimby safely home, I texted him again but got no answer. It was after ten o'clock, and he might have already been de-dea-dead…"

Brenda started really blubbering then, and Pepper handed her some tissues. She was probably hoping Brenda would use those to blow her nose instead of the embroidered napkin.

"Anyway… I can't help but think that if I'd only gone over there to visit him instead of helping Mrs. Q, Jack might be alive today."

A waterfall of fresh tears started, and Pepper patted her arm. "There now, you weren't to know. Besides, if you were there, then you might have been hurt also."

Brenda blubbered for a minute or so, and when her tears slowed, I asked one final question. "Did you see anything unusual that night? Either before the knitting class or when you were driving Mrs. Quimby around? Anyone out of place or anyone lurking about the card shop?"

Brenda shook her head, twisting the tissue in her hand. "No. Just Duane closing up his shop, but that wasn't unusual. Anyway, I've told the police all this, but I'm afraid it's not very helpful." She sighed and plumped the pillow on the end of the couch. "I'm sorry, but all this crying has me tuckered out. If you don't mind, I'd like to take a little nap."

"Of course," I said.

We got her settled on the couch. I lifted her feet then tucked a green-and-orange knitted afghan—probably one of her own creations—around her while Pepper picked up the tea implements. By the time we let ourselves out the front door, Brenda was snoring, her deep sleep helped along by the relaxation effects of Pepper's special tea, no doubt.

"So, no matching lipstick?" Pepper asked when we were back in her car and heading toward our shops on Main Street.

"Nope. I wasn't brave enough to search her bedroom, but nothing in the bathroom."

"I guess we didn't find much out," Pepper said. "But at least Gus is asking the right questions, according to what Brenda said."

"Yeah, that's great, but the question is... what is she doing about the answers?"

When I got back to my shop, I zipped off a text to Striker, filling him in on our visit to Brenda and how she'd been working on the case. I was sure they'd checked the trash for clues, too, but figured I should cover all the bases just in case.

An email arrived stating the book I'd ordered for the bartender was on its way, and it reminded me of the uncharacteristically nice things my sister had said about me and that she had faith in me finding the book.

She was the only family I had left, and I was of the mind that sisters should stick together. I was more determined than ever to help Gus find Jack's killer. Too bad I didn't have any leads. I still hadn't exhausted all the people I wanted to question, though. There were the knitting club attendees, though I felt the chances of them having noticed anything were slim. There was one person who kept cropping up and who would have been in a perfect position to see anything out of the ordinary. Duane Crosby.

Traffic in the bookstore was light, so I decided to head over to Duane's store and find out. Besides, I could use an ice cream.

Duane and his wife, Anne, were both in the store. Anne looked a bit worse for wear. Her pale face, devoid of makeup, appeared almost ghostly in contrast to her dark-red hair. She seemed a little shaky. No wonder since a murder had just happened next door.

"Willa," Duane said, raising his hand in greeting. "What can we do for you today?"

"I'll take a small chocolate chip in a waffle cone." I handed over the money to Anne and waited for Duane to scoop out the ice cream.

After he handed it over, I leaned against the ice cream cooler and took a few licks of the creamy confection. "Terrible business at Jack's."

Duane's eyes darted in the direction of the card shop. "Yeah, it's awful."

Anne chewed her lip and nodded. "Scary."

"Good thing you weren't here late that night." I took a bite from the ice cream while watching the two of them closely.

"We close around seven most nights now that summer is over," Duane said.

"Did you see or hear anything suspicious earlier? I heard someone stole his bank deposit and was wondering if the thief is watching to see our routines." I made the question sound like I was concerned for all of the merchants on Main Street, including myself, which I was.

"Nope. Can't say I've seen anyone, but then, I wasn't looking before. I was home by the time all of that went down." Duane busied himself by washing out the ice cream scoop. "Jack's place was still open when I left."

"Interesting." I crunched into the waffle cone. "Because Mrs. Quimby said she saw you around here at about the time her knitting class let out at nine p.m."

Duane's expression suddenly shifted from nervous to sad. He shook his head. "Poor Mrs. Q. I feel so bad for her. She's starting to lose it, you know? Can't remember very well at all anymore. Mixes the days up and so on. Even forgets the patterns for the knitting class and has to change the project on the fly. Wife gets upset about that." He gestured toward a canvas tote bag on the floor, out of which stuck some knitting needles. A large triangular section of something knitted in a pretty lavender yarn hung over the edge. "All the shop owners have been trying to help her out when we can."

"Really? You think she would forget something that

happened on a night someone was murdered?" I wasn't sure if I believed that or not. Was Duane lying about being here, or was Mrs. Quimby confused? But hadn't Brenda said she'd seen Duane that night too?

"Listen, Willa. I'm telling you, I was not here that night. I was at home, right, dear?" He looked over at Anne, who nodded. A bit too vigorously, in my opinion.

"Yep," she said. "We were both at home."

"We were watching *Castle* reruns that night, right?" Duane said to Anne.

"I thought that was the night before." Anne frowned then shook it off. "I can't quite remember exactly what was on TV, but we were both watching TV that night. I'd gone to the knitting class and then straight home. I remember specifically because, when I found out the next day, I thought if only we were here that night instead of watching TV, maybe we could have prevented it."

Anne started sobbing, and Duane patted her shoulder to comfort her. He scowled at me, apparently angry that I'd upset his wife. "Any more questions?"

"No, not right now," I said, heading for the exit. "Thanks."

But as I crossed the street back to the bookstore, I couldn't shake the discouraging feeling I'd just run into another dead end. I guess I'd been hoping that either Duane was the killer or he'd seen something. But other than the stolen bank deposit, which really couldn't have been a lot of money, what would his motive have been?

As I unlocked my shop, I realized Gus had been right about one thing all along. Investigating a crime was better left to the professionals. Figuring out who murdered Jack was going to be a lot harder than I'd originally thought.

BACK IN THE BOOKSTORE, I was entering the new stock into the inventory system on my computer when I heard a loud hiss from Pandora.

"What's wrong with you—"

The bells above the front entrance chimed, and the door opened.

Felicity Bates strode in, wearing a gauzy orange dress and bright-red lipstick, which clashed with the pink leash attached to Fluff.

Pandora leaped out of her bed, and she and Fluff entered into a loud hissing match.

Felicity yanked on the leash and gave her pet an irritated glare. "Stop that!"

The fluffy white-haired cat stalked over to sit near her feet but kept looking back at Pandora with an evil glare. Not to be intimidated, Pandora trotted over and took a seat near my toes, staring right back at the ill-mannered new arrivals.

Ha! I thought, resisting the urge to cheer for my pet and do some hissing myself at Felicity. So odd that she'd come in here, considering we weren't on good terms after I'd had Felicity's son arrested for murder. To be perfectly honest, I'd actually thought Felicity was the killer back then. Perhaps she had been, and she'd returned to her old ways now.

I crossed my arms and gave her a polite smile that was totally fake. "Looking for a book today?" I asked her. "I didn't know you could read."

She stared visual daggers at me. "I read just fine, Wilhelmina Chance. I also hear just fine too. And from what I've heard, you've been running around Mystic Notch, practically accusing me of killing Jack McDougall."

Her tone was steeped in pure menace, but I refused to be intimidated. I raised my chin. "Well, if the shoe fits..."

"You have no idea what you're talking about." She jabbed a long red fingernail at my face. "Listen to me, Wilhelmina Chance. I didn't kill him. In fact, I came here looking for Eddie to tell him my alibi." She gave a haughty sniff and looked me up and down, her expression dripping with disdain. "I don't know why he hangs around in here so much. This place is a dump. Just like you."

I clenched my fists to keep from smacking her. And since when did she call Striker Eddie? *I* didn't even call him Eddie. I took a deep breath and forced myself to calm down. She was trying to get me ruffled. I knew that. It would be foolish to take the bait. "Well, as you can see, *Eddie* isn't here. But you have an alibi?"

"Of course." She shined those red nails of hers on the front of her dress. "It's the best alibi anyone could have."

Sure it was. I swallowed my sarcasm and said instead, "Oh, really? What is it?"

Felicity wrinkled her nose at me. "As if I'd tell you. I'll just make sure to see *Eddie* later." She reached into a hidden pocket in her flowing dress and pulled out a business card, which she slapped down on my counter. "Have him contact me at that number, and I'll tell him everything he needs to know."

I made no move to pick it up as she started out of the store.

She stopped halfway to the door and turned back to face me. "You better watch yourself, Willa. Stop trying to play amateur detective. You have no idea what you're up against."

As the door slammed closed behind Felicity and her obnoxious pet, Pandora gave a mournful meow. I bent down and picked her up to comfort her, staring out the large front window at Felicity and her cat trotting off down the street like they didn't have a care in the world. She flicked her long red hair over her shoulder at the same time that cat of hers flicked his tail, and I snorted.

Two of a kind, that pair. Both despicable.

18

A fter Felicity left, I was too upset to think about inventory, so I called Striker instead. He answered on the first ring.

"I was just going to call you," he said, a smile in his voice. "Find anything interesting today?"

My heart squeezed with warmth that he'd been just about to call me. I liked the idea that he'd been thinking about me more than I cared to admit. But we had a case to solve here, and I needed to focus.

"I'm fine," I said, putting Pandora down then walking behind the counter. I wanted to tell him more about my visit with Brenda McDougall and Duane Crosby, but even more than that, I wanted to ask about Felicity. It wasn't that I was jealous. Just curious, that was all. I tucked the business card under the corner of the cash register, figuring I would decide whether or not to give it to him later. "So, guess who just came in here. Felicity Bates."

"Really?" He sounded surprised. "What did she want?"

"To get in my face about Jack's case. Apparently, she's heard that I've been poking around, asking questions. She said she'd heard rumors that I thought she killed Jack."

"Jeez," Striker said, sighing. "I'm sorry. She can be a real pest sometimes. You didn't actually say that to anyone, though, right?"

"Of course not," I snapped, annoyed now. Had I said that? I was sure I hadn't used those exact words. "But Sarah Delaney did say she'd seen Felicity lurking around the lamp shop the night it was broken into. And since Gus doesn't seem to want to follow up on it, I've been talking to some of the other shopkeepers to see if they saw her too. That's all."

"And have they?" Striker asked.

"Umm... well, no."

"Hmm." His long exhale echoed over the phone line. "Maybe it's a false lead, then. Gus might've known that or followed up in some other way."

I bristled. Was he sticking up for Felicity? I wanted to ask.

Before I could, though, Striker asked, "Do you have anything else?"

Forcing myself to relax, I told him about my meeting that morning. "Pepper and I paid a condolence call to Brenda McDougall. I checked her bathroom, too, but she didn't have any red lipstick, like the kind that was found on Jack's collar." I leaned my hips back against the counter and crossed my arms again. "Brenda did confirm, though, that Duane would know when Jack made his deposits."

"Good. I'll investigate that aspect and see if Duane was having any money troubles."

"Okay." The knot between my shoulder blades eased a tad, now that we were back on more comfortable ground. "I stopped in his store on my way back from meeting with Brenda too. His alibi for the night Jack died was that he was at home watching TV with his wife. Anne corroborated it."

"Interesting," Striker said. His tone shifted to concern. "Listen, Willa. I want you to be careful. I don't want you putting yourself in danger. If anything happened to you..." His words trailed off, and warmth flooded my system once more.

"Are you coming over tonight?" I asked, hoping to see him.

"I'm afraid not," he said, sounding disappointed. "I'm busy on another case, so I can't make it. Will you be all right?"

"Oh, I'll be fine." I kept my voice light despite the

disappointment I was feeling. Not only would I miss Striker's company, but it looked like I would be dining on leftover pizza for dinner.

LATER THAT NIGHT, Pandora waited patiently while Willa chowed down on cold pizza and puttered around the house. She needed to get to the barn but didn't want Willa to know she'd left the house. After what seemed like an eternity, Willa cleaned up her dishes and started upstairs, pausing in the living room to glance at the paperweight on the coffee table.

"Meow." Pandora pushed thoughts about the paperweight toward Willa. It was no ordinary trinket. Inside that glass orb, one could see answers to questions. But only if one focused clearly and believed. That was why Pandora always tried so hard to call Willa's attention to the bauble. Unfortunately, Willa wasn't quite ready to believe.

Willa walked over to the coffee table and picked up the paperweight. She held it up to the window to capture the moonlight. Pandora held her breath as Willa gazed into its depths. Then Willa shrugged and laughed, putting it back and turning to Pandora. "That's silly to think something meaningful is inside there, right?"

"Meow."

"Also silly to talk to my cat." Willa turned off the living room lights and headed up to her room, the third stair creaking in the usual spot.

Pandora followed her up and waited patiently, curled up at the foot of the bed, feigning sleep as Willa did her nightly ritual. Finally, once Willa was tucked under the down comforter and snoring, Pandora trotted back down the stairs and out into the night.

She raced down the path to Elspeth's barn. All the other cats were already assembled when she arrived.

"I had the most awful encounter today," Pandora said, trotting to stand in front of a hay bale between Inkspot and Kelly. "Fluff came into the bookstore along with that terrible owner of his. Right in my territory! Very upsetting."

"Were you able to find anything out from him?" Otis asked, giving her a sly stare. "I don't like the idea of him running all over town on his own, digging up who knows what."

"I didn't get anything new. He mostly just put on a show for his owner, hissing and acting very impolite," Pandora said. "But he did tell me before that he investigates without his human. I don't like it either. He could get up to something really sneaky because cats can go places humans can't, and no one pays any attention to them snooping around. Thankfully, Fluff's not that smart, so I doubt he'll find anything."

"What about the police case?" Tigger asked. "Anyone heard anything new on that?"

"No," Sasha meowed. "I don't think there's been much progress at all."

"Let's go over what we do know, then," Snowball suggested.

"Good idea." Inkspot stood and began to pace the inside of the circle they'd formed. "We know the break-ins are related to the ingredients."

"Yes." Hope sat up. "And we also know that Sarah and Felicity have been trying to locate them."

"They must not be having any luck." Otis gave a derisive snort. "Because they're still looking in the same area."

"One good thing, Elspeth has made the tea that will hopefully counteract the hex on Gus," Truffles offered. "I heard her say she's going to drop it off at the bookstore tomorrow. She seems to think that Willa will have a better chance of persuading Gus to drink it."

"Good. Good." Inkspot stopped and sat at the center of the circle. "What about this hex, then? Who could have cast it?"

"Felicity and Sarah both claim to be witches," Otis said. "My vote is with them. And since we know they are looking for the ingredients, they wouldn't want Gus to investigate too thoroughly."

"But why would they be looking inside the stores?"

Sasha asked. "The buildings weren't even here in Hester Warren's time."

Inkspot's tail twitched as they all considered the question. "Perhaps someone dug the ingredients up at a later date and hid them inside."

"It's possible," Otis said. "Three hundred years have gone by."

"Whoever hexed Gus would have had to make her drink the hex potion a couple of times," Pandora said. "Her personality is strong. It would take a lot to make her change."

"True." Kelly shuddered. "Reminds me of those vaccines my owner makes me get at the vet's office. Booster shots, they call them."

"Yes, Gus must have needed more than one dose for the hex to truly take effect." Hope glanced over at Pandora. "Makes sense. She is contrary, as you say."

"So it would have to be someone Gus trusted, which leaves Felicity and Sarah out," Kelly said. "Let's not forget there are others who wish ill on the town."

"Indeed. We must not slack off on our end of the investigation," Inkspot said. "The clues are confusing, and one person is already dead. I don't want another human murdered on our watch."

"Agreed," the cats said.

"I'm no fan of Felicity Bates," Pandora said, frowning. "And I don't really know Sarah Delaney all that well, but

I just don't understand why either of them would murder Jack McDougall."

"Perhaps it was an accident," Sasha said. "We know both of them were looking for the ingredients. Maybe one of them went into his store, looking for them, and he caught them by surprise."

"That still doesn't explain why Jack's dead, though," Pandora said. "Why kill him, when they could've just knocked him out with a spell or a hex? Or better yet, wait until the store was empty to go in and search, like they did with the other break-ins?" She shook her head then stood and stretched. "It makes no sense."

"Maybe the spell went awry, and he ended up dead," Kelly suggested.

"We all know they aren't the sharpest broomsticks in the closet," Sasha said.

"True," Pandora agreed. "But we might also want to broaden our suspect list. My human has other suspicions. She's been talking to Duane and Anne Crosby and Mrs. Quimby at the yarn shop."

Snowball gasped. "Surely she doesn't suspect Mrs. Q! She's a nice old lady."

Pandora shrugged. "Wouldn't be the first time the one who seemed least likely ended up being the killer."

"I'd rather see it be that Crosby character. He never lets us lick the ice cream remnants out of the containers.

Locks them right up in that trash bin out back. Such a waste," Sasha said.

"He *would* know all about Jack's bank deposit routine," Inkspot added.

"And what about the wife?" Tigger purred. "I heard from Elvira, the cat at the library, that she was in the alley, rummaging in the trash."

"Investigating herself because Gus isn't doing such a great job, I'm afraid," Pandora said.

"None of this bodes well. I have to wonder if there are multiple motives involved here. We need Gus's help. I think our main priority is making sure she drinks that potion from Elspeth. It's good that Elspeth is dropping it off at the bookstore." Inkspot turned to Pandora. "We're counting on you to use all of your powers of persuasion to get her to drink it."

19

By midmorning the next day, I'd finally finished logging my new inventory into the system and was stocking and reshelving things while discussing Jack's case with Pandora. I knew it was silly, but she was a good listener. Besides, if I didn't pay too close attention, it almost seemed like she would nod in agreement at things or meow in response. Anyway, business was slow again, and I needed someone to talk to.

"I don't know how exactly, Pandora," I said, shoving a heavy volume of Shakespeare's classics back into the top row. "But Felicity Bates is involved in all of this somehow."

Pandora meowed loudly.

"Right." I picked up a stack of atlases and carried them to the map section. "Gus did have a point about

Felicity being rich. She doesn't need the money, so why would she steal Jack's bank deposit?"

Pandora hopped up on the bookshelf where I was working and cocked her head to the side.

"Makes no sense, right?" I sighed. "And what about the lipstick on Jack's collar? Brenda wasn't wearing that shade. In fact, when I checked her bathroom drawers yesterday, I didn't find any lipstick at all. Only clear lip gloss."

I leaned back slightly to see around the end of the row I was working in. From this angle, I could just see Jack's card shop down the street. The crime scene tape was still crisscrossing the door.

"I feel bad for Brenda McDougall," I told Pandora as we walked back toward the counter. "She was a victim here too. Now she's a widow, and since Gus is being a slacker, she's trying to find her husband's killer, and he might very well have been having an affair." Pandora hissed, and I smiled. "I agree. Not nice of him at all. I don't think Brenda knew... or did she?"

New suspicions formed in my head. "If she did, would that make her mad enough to kill? But then why investigate?"

"Meow."

"Right. She has an alibi. She was helping Mrs. Quimby find her car. And Mrs. Quimby corroborated that she did forget where her car was."

Shaking my head, I went back behind the counter again. I now had two reasons to solve this case. To help my sister and to help Brenda. Now, if only I could get Jack's ghost to be more helpful and answer my questions, I would be all set. I doubted that would happen, though. Most likely he had ghost amnesia, an affliction of the newly dead. Still, I couldn't help but feel he was holding back something from me during our previous two conversations. Then again, that could've been guilt over his infidelity.

Just then the bells above my door jangled, and Elspeth walked in, carrying a large mason jar filled with yellow liquid that looked like ginger tea, my sister's favorite childhood drink.

"Hello, dear," she greeted me, her smile sweet and kindly. "You said Gus was feeling under the weather, so I made her favorite tea. She can drink it hot, cold, or luke-warm. It's good for what ails her, you know. And we can't have our sheriff getting sick, with this crime spree in town. Anyway, I figured I could drop it off here, and you could give it to her later. The sheriff's office is out of my way. Don't worry about leaving it out. It won't go bad." Elspeth set the jar on the counter then stepped back. "Just make sure she drinks all of it. That's very important. It should help her get back to her old self. Promise me, dear."

"I promise. I'll do my best." I eyed the jar, skeptical

that a drink was going to help Gus. Elspeth was so sweet, though, I didn't want to burst her bubble. She'd been kind enough to make the tea and bring it here, and I would see that Gus got it. Getting my sister to drink it all was another matter, but it was the thought that counted. I doubted the drink would make her start acting like the old Gus again.

"And how's my beautiful Pandora?" Elspeth asked, walking to the window and bending to pat the preening cat's head. She stayed there, stooped over, for several long moments as Pandora purred loudly.

Elspeth straightened finally and waved as she left, making me promise once more to make sure Gus drank all of the tea. It struck me as odd that she was so insistent about it. My thoughts went to the old cookbook that wasn't really a cookbook at all on Elspeth's counter. Was there something extra special about that tea?

Honestly, I'd never believed in magic at all before I'd moved to Mystic Notch, but now that I'd been here awhile, I was starting to rethink things. I'd seen enough strange occurrences in my time here to make even the most fervent critic a convert.

I stared at the jar of tea and exhaled slowly. It wasn't like Gus could get any more messed up than she already was, so yeah, I would do my best to make sure she drank it all. I set the jar beneath the counter until my sister dropped by again. She'd been coming into the bookstore pretty regularly lately, so hopefully today would be no exception.

PANDORA HAD PRETENDED to be napping in her bed by the window while Elspeth was in the store, but once the older woman left, she lazily stretched and looked at the jar of tea and considered how she could best help Willa get Gus to drink all of it.

Pandora started her grooming routine while she thought about that, but a few minutes into it, she got a tingly feeling, and her hairs stood on end. She looked out the window to see Felicity and Fluff walking down the other side of the street. As if on cue, Fluff turned to smirk straight at her, the sequins on that ridiculous pink harness of his glowing in the sun. Pandora growled and looked away to find Sarah Delaney coming out of a nearby side street with her Yorkie, Skeezits, on a leash. Ha! Served Fluff right. He'd been so busy smirking at Pandora, he'd not seen the little dog.

Yip! Yip! Yip!

Pandora laughed as Fluff jerked sideways in shock then tucked and rolled on the sidewalk, getting tangled up in his pink harness and leash. What an idiot. Tufts of his white hair went flying everywhere and...

Wait!

Eyes wide, Pandora's mind began to swirl with a new idea. White hairs. White hairs.

Of course. The picture that Striker had shown Willa the other night from the robbery. Those hairs in the photo weren't blond. They were from Fluff. That proved that Fluff, and likely Felicity, were behind the break-ins.

Outside, Sarah gave Felicity a dirty look and jerked the tiny Yorkie away from the bigger cat. The two women gave each other a wide berth as they continued on in opposite directions.

Soon, Gus came out of Jack's card store, and Pandora's hopes soared. Maybe she'd been investigating, finally. She glanced back at the jar on the counter. If they could get Gus to drink all of Elspeth's tea, she would be doing a lot more than just investigating. Determined, Pandora meowed loudly. She would do everything she could to force the human sheriff to drink it then find a way to make Gus reevaluate the hairs from the crime scene.

Gus headed toward her squad car, parked at the curb, and Pandora closed her eyes, willing her to come to the bookstore instead, her whiskers twitching and her kinked tail swishing back and forth in concentration.

Finally, Gus stopped and turned slowly, her gaze narrowed on Last Chance Books. She started toward the bookshop, and Pandora filled with satisfaction. It worked! Good. Her powers of persuasion were getting stronger. Now, if she could just use them to get Gus to drink the tea...

The sheriff came into the store and plopped down on one of the purple microsuede sofas near the front of the place. Pandora walked over and hopped up on the counter to stand in front of Willa, over where she'd stored the jar of tea on the shelf beneath, hoping to remind her to push it on her sister.

Willa for once, however, did not seem to need the reminder. She reached down and pulled out the jar, then twisted the top off an insulated stainless-steel tumbler, filled it halfway with ice from her mini-fridge, and poured the concoction inside. Willa took a seat in the armchair adjacent to the sofa where her sister sat and held out the drink. "Hey, sis. Elspeth stopped by earlier with a jar of your favorite iced tea. Here."

Gus took the cup and sniffed it, grimacing. "I haven't had any of this since I was a kid."

"I know, right? So considerate of her to make it for you," Willa said. "Go ahead and try some."

"Nah." Gus tried to hand her back the cup. "I'm not really thirsty right now."

Pandora jumped up next to Gus and nudged her outstretched arm, concentrating hard again, trying to get her to drink the stuff. But no dice.

When Willa didn't take the cup, Gus set it on the coffee table then sat back. "I'm really only here killing time. I'm supposed to be working on the robbery and Jack's murder case, but hey, things will happen when they happen. A good investigation can't be rushed."

Willa gave an exasperated sigh and shook her head. "Speaking of the case, have you talked to Duane Crosby yet? From what I've heard, he would've known about the bank deposits Jack made. He claims he was home the night Jack died, though, watching TV with his wife and—"

"You know, Willa," Gus said, holding up a hand to stop her. "I'm just really not that interested in any of this. Since when did you become such a bore, sis? Always harping on about crimes."

"Well, a man has been killed." Willa's tone indicated she was a bit disturbed at her sister's lack of urgency and empathy. Pandora couldn't blame her, though she knew the real reason.

"Right and having my sister go around town, accusing people, isn't helping. I have a list of suspects. I've talked to the Crosbys. I've had tea with Mrs. Q, talked to the women from her knitting class, and yes, I have looked in the trash behind the stores." Gus gave Willa a pointed look. "Is there anything else I should look into?"

Pandora jumped from the sofa to the coffee table, pushing the cup of tea closer to Gus with her nose, but the human wasn't catching on. Ugh. Perhaps she should try to get the hint about the hairs across. Gus hadn't even mentioned interrogating Felicity in the little speech she'd just given. She hopped to the floor and twined around Gus's ankles, leaving a trail of cat hair on the cuffs of her dark-brown pants. But again, Gus still remained oblivious.

"Welp, I need to go," Gus said, standing.

"Wait! Don't you at least want to try your tea? Elspeth went through all the trouble of making it for you, and I just put fresh ice in." Willa picked up the tumbler again and held it out to her sister. "Please?"

"Fine." Gus snatched the tumbler from Willa, her expression annoyed. "Do you have a cover? I'll take this with me and drink it later, okay? Stop bugging me."

Willa screwed the cover onto the tumbler, and Gus left. Willa slumped down on the couch. Her aura shifted from a hopeful bright blue to a darker indigo. Not good. She was depressed. Pandora jumped up into the chair with her, thinking that even though Gus hadn't picked up on the clue about the hairs, Willa might. She needed to redeem herself for failing to persuade Gus to drink the tea. If she could get Willa to clue in to the hairs, at least she would have made some progress.

She rubbed against Willa's black T-shirt, making sure to leave as many hairs on the fabric as possible. Though not as noticeable as white, the grays stood out nicely.

With a sigh, Willa stroked Pandora's fur then began

brushing off her pants. "You're a good kitty, but I really need to invest in a lint roller company when you..."

Willa's voice trailed off as she plucked one of the hairs from her shirt and held it up to the light. Realization dawned in her eyes, and her aura brightened up to a sparkling yellow. Pandora purred with satisfaction as her human got it.

"Hey!" Willa glanced over at Pandora. "This reminds me of the hairs found at the burglary scene. They were only a bit longer than this, and I thought they were short for human hair. I thought they were blond, too, but maybe they were white. White like Felicity Bates's cat."

20

W hen Pepper stopped by later that afternoon, I was bursting to tell her about my cat hair theory, but I had a lot of other things to fill her in on first. She'd brought tea and cinnamon scones, so we made ourselves comfortable on the sofas, and I nibbled a scone while she poured tea.

"I saw Elspeth." Pepper's green eyes assessed me over the rim of her teacup. "She said she made a special drink for Gus to perk her up a bit."

I nodded. "I gave it to her, but she'll probably just toss it out. Anyway, I don't think a simple tea is going to fix her." Was it? A quick glance at my friend told me that she disagreed.

"Oh, you'd be surprised. Elspeth's concoctions have an effect on people. Sort of like how my teas have effects," Pepper said.

Okay, she had a point. I used to doubt Pepper's claim that her tea had magical effects, but I'd seen it in action firsthand. Maybe I should just have faith in Elspeth's tea. Maybe I should just believe. I might regret wishing for Gus's recovery because my sister and I could butt heads sometimes, especially when it came to investigating the crimes of Mystic Notch, but anything would be better than the muted version of Gus we had now.

"I hope it does help," Pepper continued. "Gus has been so lackadaisical about her work these days."

"Tell me about it. I've had to fill in for her. Did I tell you I stopped by Duane's shop to talk to him about his whereabouts the night of Jack's murder?" I asked.

"Nope." A customer came in and began browsing the shelves. Pepper leaned closer to me, lowering her voice. "What did he have to say for himself?"

"Well, Duane says he was home that night, watching TV. His wife corroborated his story."

"Interesting." Pepper frowned. "Would Anne do that if she thought her husband was a killer?"

"I honestly don't know them well enough to say one way or another." I smiled at the new arrival as he passed. "Can I help you find anything today?"

"No, no. I'm just looking, thanks," the older gentleman said, disappearing down another row of books.

I turned back to Pepper. "Anyway, Duane doesn't matter because I have a better suspect in mind."

"Really? Who?"

"Felicity Bates."

"Well, we already know she's suspicious, but what do you have that ties her to the crimes? I know Gus seems to think she is not involved."

"And she claims to have an alibi… one that she will only give to Striker."

"What? How do you know that?"

"She stopped by here, hoping to see him." I took a sip of soothing tea. Just the memory of her haughty attitude when she was in here made me angry. "That's why I think she's up to something. She was too smug. Too insistent."

Pepper frowned. "So did she tell Striker what her alibi was?"

"No. At least I don't think so. I told him about her visit, but he didn't seem very eager to talk to her." I was sure he would fill me in once he did. I leaned closer, lowering my voice. "But this is why I think she is more involved than she is letting on. Striker showed me photos from the crime scene the other night, and one of those photos showed a few blond hairs left behind at the lamp store break-in."

Pepper frowned. "Uh… news flash, Felicity isn't blond."

"Right. But what if the hairs weren't human hairs?"

"What else would they be?" Pepper scrunched her nose.

"Fur." I glanced around to make sure no one was listening to our conversation. I wouldn't put it past Felicity to have spies out in the neighborhood. "From that long-haired white cat of hers."

"Fluff?" Pepper stepped back, her expression thoughtful. "You really think Felicity would bring her pet to a break-in?"

"Why not?" I shrugged. "She takes him everywhere else with her."

"True. And that cat does have long hair. I suppose it could look like strands from a human with short hair, but were any hairs found at the murder scene?"

"Not that I know of," I said. "But then, with my sister acting the way she's been lately, who knows if her investigation was thorough?"

"Wow." Pepper said. "If you're correct, that could change everything. But we still need to convince Gus that it's worth pursuing."

"Striker said she'd sent the hairs to the lab. They'd be able to tell if the hairs are human or feline. Hopefully, Gus will drink that tea soon and be alert enough to put two and two together when those results come in."

The customer who had been perusing the shelves came to the register with a couple of hardcover novels, and I excused myself to ring him up. He left, and I hurried back to the sofa.

"There's another person we might suspect too," Pepper said.

"Who?"

"Brenda McDougall."

"The grieving widow? But she seemed so upset, plus she has an alibi, and besides, she's investigating it herself. Why would she do that if she were the killer?"

"Good point. Still, if Jack was having an affair and she knew about it, that would give her a powerful motive for murder." Pepper sipped her tea.

"Okay, I'll give you that, but what about her claim that she was driving Mrs. Quimby around at the time of the murder? And she had the socks from the knitting class, so we know she was there."

"Maybe we should double-check with Mrs. Quimby on that." Pepper put her empty cup down and started putting the tea items back in her quilted bag. "I mean, don't you think it's odd Brenda was looking in the trash? Why look there?"

"It's almost as if she expected to find something in particular there."

"Or didn't want the police to find something that had been thrown out earlier."

I blinked at her a few times as a new theory occurred. "What if she had a reason and just didn't mention it to us? What if Brenda knew something was in the trash? If she didn't find it, like she said, then it might still be there."

Pepper put the last saucer in the bag and zipped it up. "They haven't picked up the trash yet this week."

"All righty then," I said, pushing up from the couch and flipping the store sign to closed. "I say we get on over there and see what we can find."

21

It was broad daylight, but I didn't want anyone to see us lurking in the alley. Being a small town, Mystic Notch wasn't exactly brimming with traffic or pedestrians, so it was easy to run across the street when no one was looking. We hugged the sides of the building all the way up to the narrow alley that led to the area behind the shops.

I'd been in such a hurry that I hadn't noticed Pandora following us out the door. Oh, well. It was too late to go back now. I could hear the grinding of the trash trucks in the distance and the boom of dumpsters as they were emptied then dropped back onto the ground. If we didn't go through this stuff now, it would be too late. Hopefully Pandora would stick by my side, as she usually did when we walked over to Elspeth's.

The small area behind Jack's store housed the dumpsters and trash bins for many of the stores on the block and had extra parking. It was set up in a square with stores on three sides. It smelled like sour milk, and the pavement around the dumpsters could only be described as greasy. Yech. I was just wondering which one of us would be tasked with jumping in the dumpster when I spied a sign for the back door to Jack's shop. Thankfully he didn't have a dumpster. Just four over-sized trash bins.

"Over here!" I pointed, and we scurried over, each opening a bin and starting our search.

Pandora was more interested in the dumpster over by the fish market. I tried to shoo her away, but she just shot me one of her don't-tell-me-what-to-do glares. I didn't have time to mess around, so I decided to ignore her and focus on the task at hand.

Luckily Jack's trash bin didn't have any food in it. Just paper. I dug deep, pawing through old photocopies of sports cards, invoices, and receipts. I didn't find anything that even remotely resembled a clue. Pepper had already moved to her second barrel by the time I was done with my first, so I picked up the pace.

"Look!" Pepper said, holding up a dark-blue pouch. "It's a bank deposit pouch with the name of Jack's store!"

I rushed over as she unzipped it. It was empty.

"You think the killer took the money out and then tossed the pouch in the trash?" I asked.

Pepper's brow creased. "Why would they do that? You'd think they'd be in a hurry and just grab the envelope and run."

"Maybe they didn't want to get caught with it?" I suggested. "Or maybe they got the money from Jack before he died. They could have fought over it somehow, and Jack could have gotten killed in the process."

"Then how would the bag get in the trash?" Pepper asked. "Surely the police wouldn't have just thrown it out. I'm sure that even in Gus's current state, she would take this in as evidence." Pepper held the bag by the corner, presumably so she wouldn't mess up any fingerprints.

"Meow." Pandora sat on the trash bin next to the one Pepper had pulled the bag from watching us with those unsettling golden-green eyes.

"Do you think that's why his ghost is being so evasive?" I ignored the cat. "Maybe he was up to more than just an affair."

"Merow!" Pandora was louder this time.

"Not sure." Pepper went back to digging. "Maybe there is another clue."

We tried to get on with the search, but Pandora interrupted us by jumping from one can to the next, meowing loudly and lifting her head skyward. I glanced up to see the signs above the back doors. "Wait a minute. This isn't Jack's trash. It's Duane's."

"Then why is Jack's deposit envelope in here?" Pepper made a face and waved her hand in front of her nose as she opened a particularly stinky bag of trash. This one had the remnants of ice cream continuers and stunk like sour milk.

"Meow." Pandora eyed the bag and sniffed as if it contained the most delicious aroma, which, to her, it probably did.

The spoiling ice cream proved one thing. The trash can Pepper had produced the bag from definitely belonged to Duane's ice cream shop. My stomach sank to my toes as I put the clues together. "There's only one reason I can think of. Duane must be involved somehow. He tossed the bag to get rid of the evidence."

Pepper looked skeptical. "I don't know. Doesn't he have an alibi?"

"Yeah, but it's his wife."

"You think they are in it together?" Pepper whispered, glancing at Jack's back door as if he and Anne would burst out at any minute.

The thought made me nervous. "We better get Gus out here." I pulled out my cell phone and started to dial, only to stop. "I'm not sure what good it would do to tell my sister, though, since she probably won't do anything about it." I deleted the numbers I'd typed in and entered Striker's number instead. If anyone knew the urgency of our information, it was him. Except my call rang and rang and ended up going to his voicemail. I tried again. Same result. Crap. He must be busy on that other case he was working on.

After typing in a quick text to him, I shoved my phone back into my pocket and took the envelope from Pepper. "Let's get this to the sheriff's office. We have to depend on Gus now. Let's hope she drank that tea!"

22

Pepper went back to her shop, and I locked Pandora in the bookstore and then rushed to the sheriff's office, my fingers crossed that Gus would be in. Good news, she was. Bad news, she was sitting behind her desk with her feet up, listening to jazz. I walked past the receptionist's desk without stopping and made a beeline for Gus, tossing the empty deposit envelope we'd found on her desktop.

"What's this?" Gus asked, frowning.

"That's the stolen deposit envelope from when Jack was murdered," I said, crossing my arms.

"Huh." My sister picked up the envelope and looked inside it. "And you found this where?"

"In Duane's trash."

If my sister had any reaction to that news, her facial expression didn't show it. She blinked at me. "And..."

With an exasperated sigh, I threw my hands up. "And don't you want to follow up with Duane and ask why this was in his trash? Seems pretty suspicious to me. It implicates him."

"I don't think so." Gus relaxed back into her chair again. "He's got an alibi for Jack's time of death."

I wanted to yank my sister out of that chair by her shirt front and make her go, but I doubted the rest of the staff in the department would appreciate that. So, I continued to argue my point. "Duane's wife, you mean? I think there's a good chance she might be lying."

"You do, huh?" Gus gave me a perturbed stare. "Look, sis. Haven't I told you before to leave the detecting to the professionals? If I had a good lead on Jack's killer, I'd follow it. You're barking up the wrong tree with Duane. Besides, if that envelope was a clue, then you just messed up the chain of evidence."

I pursed my lips to hold back my frustration. I'll admit I'd felt a flare of hope when she nagged me about staying out of her investigations, thinking perhaps the tea had worked and the old Gus was coming back, but now I was just more irritated than ever. "You don't like my theory about Duane? Fine. How about this, then? There were hairs found at the lamp shop burglary crime scene, and I don't think they're human. I think they came from a feline."

This made my sister laugh out loud. "Seriously, Willa? You think they're cat hairs?"

"I do." My jaw tensed. "It's not funny. Why couldn't they be? There's plenty of cat owners around this town."

Gus slapped the top of her desk and chortled. "So, you expect me to believe all these crimes were committed by a cat burglar. Get it? *Cat* burglar!" She snorted. "Very funny."

"I don't find it funny at all." I squared my shoulders. "And I don't think the cat committed the crime. The owner did. Felicity Bates, in particular. She's involved in all this, somehow. I can feel it. And she's always got her cat with her, so why not take it to a crime scene too?"

Gus finally stopped laughing and gave me a flat look instead. "First Duane and now Felicity? How many more people are you going to accuse of these crimes? Who's next?"

With a sigh, I looked away. Ugh. I really should've planned out what I was going to say better than I had and not just charged over here in a hurry. My gaze snagged on the tumbler full of tea sitting on top of Gus's file cabinet. I wandered over to check, hoping to find it empty, but no. It was still as full as when it had left my shop earlier. I picked it up and set it on the desk in front of my sister. "Don't forget your drink."

"I'm not thirsty," Gus said, grumbling.

"C'mon. Elspeth's been like a second grandmother to

us. We've known her our whole lives. She made this especially for you, Augusta. The least you can do is drink it. You don't want to hurt her feelings, do you?"

My sister eyed the cup for a moment, and I held my breath. Then she pushed away from the desk and stood. "I'll drink it later. Now, if you'll excuse me, sis, I need to get ready for my gig at the Blue Moon."

DISCOURAGED, I walked back to my bookshop. I'd gotten nothing useful out of Gus at all. She'd disregarded all my clues and couldn't have cared less about my theories. Shoulders slumped, I pulled out my phone, hoping for a text from Striker, but I found only a blank black screen.

Jack's empty deposit envelope crackled in my pocket, where I'd shoved it before leaving Gus's office. It was clear Gus didn't want it for evidence, and I wasn't going to risk her throwing it out. I took it out and stared at it, replaying the moment Pepper and I had found it. I couldn't shake the feeling I was missing something there. We'd been rooting through the trash cans. The same trash cans that Brenda McDougall had been searching through a few days prior.

My posture straightened slightly. Brenda.

It seemed odd that she wouldn't have seen it when she'd been riffling through the garbage. Then again, she might not have looked in Duane's trash, just Jack's. Even if Brenda had pulled the envelope out of the trash and taken it to Gus, she most likely wouldn't have given it any credence anyway, given the reception I got today. Maybe Brenda had found it and had called Gus about it, and when she wasn't interested, Brenda just tossed it back away.

Darn.

I needed to get an explanation from Duane. Determined, I headed straight for Duane's shop again. I saw him peek out the window at me, so I knew he was there. I walked right in and cornered him behind his counter.

"Explain this to me, Duane." I smacked the envelope down in front of him. "Pepper and I found this in your trash earlier. It's the deposit from the night Jack was killed. Empty. Want to tell me how this ended up in your trash when supposedly you weren't even here?"

Duane glared at me, but I didn't break eye contact, not backing down an inch. Finally, he relented, his breath escaping in a big huff. "Fine. You're right. I was here that night. Mrs. Quimby did see me. But I didn't kill Jack. I swear."

"What were you doing in your shop after closing?" I raised a brow at him.

His face reddened, and he scowled down at the counter. "I was skulking around after Anne. She was having an affair with Jack, and I wanted to catch them in the act. Get photos with my cell phone for proof."

"Right." My suspicions hit the red zone. "Well, if Jack was sleeping with your wife, that seems all the more reason for you to want to kill him. I bet you were really upset. In a jealous rage, even. Cheating drives people crazy."

"No!" He looked up at me then, holding his hands up in surrender. "I swear I didn't touch him. Sure, I was angry, but I'm no killer. Besides, I was long gone by the time he was shot."

His tone sounded earnest enough, but I wasn't ready to buy it just yet. I hiked my chin at him. "So, if you weren't at home at the time of Jack's death, and you weren't here, then where were you?"

"At the Blue Moon," he said. "You can ask Gus, if you don't believe me. She was playing the piano and singing the blues that night."

I wanted to call him out in another lie, but darn it, I couldn't. If Anne had been having an affair with Jack McDougall, that would certainly explain why she'd acted so strangely the first time I'd been in the shop to question Duane. It would also explain why she'd been so willing to lie for her husband. Because she'd actually been with *Jack* and couldn't very well tell Duane that. She must have assumed Duane really was home and *thought* she'd been there too.

I narrowed my gaze on Duane. "And what about the envelope?"

He frowned at it. "I never touched it. If you found it in my trash, I have no idea how it got there."

A likely story. "Of course, you would say that if you were the killer. You already lied about where you were once. How do I know you aren't lying now?"

"Seriously." He picked up his cell phone and held it out to me. "Call Gus and ask her. How dumb would it be for me to lie a second time about where I was, especially if I used the town sheriff as my alibi?"

23

S till reeling over what Duane had just told me, I went back to Last Chance Books. A package was waiting for me by the front door, and I carried it inside to the counter. It was the book from California I'd ordered for the bartender. After tidying up, I called her to let her know it was ready to be picked up. She said she would stop in within the hour. I told her not to hurry. I would stay open late, if she needed.

After all, what else did I have to do? Striker must have still been busy on a case, as he hadn't returned my messages, and my little investigating into Jack's death was starting to get complicated.

I began wandering around the store, straightening books here, putting away stock there, my mind focused on the case. My enthusiasm from earlier had worn off, leaving me a bit depressed. Duane sounded so confident that Gus would vouch for him. And he was right. It would have been stupid for him to use such a lame alibi if it weren't going to pan out. My gut told me he wasn't the killer.

Honestly, I even felt a little bad for Duane. And no wonder Jack's ghost had been acting shady. He *was* hiding something—the fact he was cheating on Brenda. I walked up front to tidy the sitting area. Could Jack be hiding something else, though, as well? Like perhaps he really did know something about that night but didn't say anything because he was too busy hiding the fact he'd been having an affair with Anne. Yep. I would bet he remembered more than he was letting on.

I sank down on one of the purple sofas and glared up at the ceiling, venting all my frustrations skyward. "Jack McDougall, you show yourself right now, and tell me the truth!"

Shocked didn't begin to describe how I felt when he actually did.

His ghost appeared in a swirl of smoke and gray mist. Pandora batted at the mist with her paw.

"Well?" I asked when I'd recovered from the surprise. "What do you have to say for yourself?"

"What do you mean?" Jack's guilty swirl gave away the fact that he knew exactly what I meant.

"You've been lying to me. Covering up. You were up

to something the night you died, and it wasn't with your wife."

Jack's ghost had the decency to look sheepish. "Okay. Fine. Yes, I was having an affair with Anne Crosby. We'd met in my shop earlier that night, after I closed. Things didn't go well, though, and then I guess I was so tired later that I fell asleep in the storeroom."

I crossed my arms over my chest. "What do you mean 'things didn't go well'?"

Jack made a face. "I had to break things off with her. I mean, at first the affair was just for fun, but then she started to get clingy and demanding. She was not pleased."

Well, that was enlightening. "How mad was she?"

"Fuming," Jack said. "I was afraid she was going to stab me with those knitting needles of hers."

But Jack wasn't stabbed. He was shot with his own gun. And only someone who knew where he kept it would have had access. That deposit bag in Duane's trash might make sense after all.

"Was Anne mad enough to kill you?" I asked. "She was in the store. She had the opportunity, and I'm sure she knew where you kept the gun."

"No. No way." Jack's ghost frowned. "I clearly remember her leaving. I locked the door behind her after she went. There's no way she'd have killed me."

I exhaled slowly. Jack had dumped Anne, so I

doubted there was a reason for him to lie about the events to protect her. Quite the opposite. I would have thought he would have been mad at her and wanting revenge. "Did you see anybody else?"

"No." His ghostly brow wrinkled in concentration. "Nope. Only that fluffy white cat. It was digging around out behind the shop when Anne left."

My ears pricked up at that. "Fluffy white cat? Like the one Felicity Bates has?"

Jack made a face. "Oh, her. I don't think it was hers. It wasn't on a leash. Though I wouldn't put it past her to be lurking out there."

"Why is that?"

"She's weird. When she was in my shop, looking for tarot cards that time, she wanted me to let her look in the basement. Said she wanted to look for old stock." Jack shook his head. "Any idiot knows you don't keep sports cards in a basement. The dampness ruins them."

"So, what happened? Did you let her lo—"

Before I could finish my question, the front door of the shop opened with a jangle of bells, and Jack's ghost disappeared in a flash. Pandora hissed, and I stood, feeling a bit out of sorts, given that I was just conversing with a ghost. A despicable cheater ghost whose wife was now front and center in my store.

Of course the thought had crossed my mind that

Brenda did know about the affair and had killed him herself, but if that were the case, then why would she be investigating?

I cleared my throat and forced a smile I didn't feel. She looked so vulnerable and sad. It made my heart ache. "Brenda. Hi. Welcome to Last Chance Books. How can I help you today?"

"Hey, Willa. I thought I'd stop by and see if you'd found out anything else with my husband's case." She swiped a shaky hand through her hair. "I hate to admit it, but law enforcement doesn't seem to be doing much with the investigation into Jack's death, and time is running out. I watch all those detective shows on TV. I know that after so much time, leads go cold."

"Oh, um..." I wasn't quite ready to share what I'd learned yet, especially since I hadn't even had a chance to hash it all out with Striker, not to mention there was a possibility that Brenda was the killer. "I haven't really found much, I'm afraid."

"Anything? Anything at all?" she pleaded, her tone growing more desperate. "I'd be interested in any leads at all, even dubious ones. I have my own suspicions..."

So did I. "The case is still ongoing. As far as I know, the police are looking into a few things. I just wouldn't want to tell you something, then have you be disappointed if it turns out to be nothing."

Brenda leaned closer. "It's Duane Crosby, isn't it? He was acting awfully squirrelly when I talked to him the other day."

"No." We were treading on dangerous ground indeed, and the last thing I needed was to get caught up in an affair debacle. Still, I needed to give her something. "Duane's not the killer."

She frowned. "How do you know?"

"He has an alibi."

"Oh." She seemed dejected, and we sat there in silence as she sipped the water. Finally she sighed. "I have to confess something."

I was all ears. "What?"

"I found something at the store after the police left that I think might be evidence, but I was too embarrassed to turn it in." She looked down at the floor, unable to meet my eyes.

"What was it?"

"Some red hairs. They were on the floor near the back door. I was cleaning up the mess from whoever broke the lock." She pressed her lips together, fresh tears streaking her cheeks. "See, I think Jack might have been having an af-aff-affair."

Her shoulders shook, and I reached for the tissues. After much sniffling, she wiped her eyes.

So, she *did* know about the affair. That gave her

motive to kill, but if she were the killer, would she be confessing this all to me now? And she did seem appropriately upset. Unless the reason she was so upset was that she might get caught.

Once she'd composed herself, she looked up. "See, that's why I suspected Duane. I think the woman Jack was messing around with was Anne Crosby."

"And you figured he might have been jealous."

She nodded. "Are you sure about the alibi?"

I hadn't asked Gus yet, but I was fairly certain Duane wouldn't lie about the alibi, as it would be too easy for us to find out. The direction of the conversation reminded me of how we'd found the deposit slip in his trash but no other clues. "Did you find anything when you looked out in the trash behind your husband's store?"

She shook her head. "I saw the red hairs while cleaning up, like I told you, and I thought something else might be out there, but I didn't find anything."

Brenda finished her water and pushed up from the couch. "Well, I just hope this gets solved soon." She gave me a pleading look. "Will you let me know if you find out anything else? I'll leave you my cell number."

"Of course. You can count on me." We exchanged contact info, and I pushed her out the door and retreated into my shop to process the new information I'd discovered from Brenda, Duane, and Jack's ghost.

The bartender still hadn't shown up yet, so I took a seat again to chat with Pandora. Except she wasn't there. I searched her bed and all the chairs. Even went back into the storeroom, but no cat. I went back up front and flopped down on the sofa, brushing away a few stray gray cat hairs. I thought about the fact that Jack had just said he'd seen a white cat the night he'd died, and Felicity had wanted to poke around in his basement. I was positive that white cat was Fluff and Felicity was involved in all this.

Brenda had found red hairs near the door. Both Felicity and Anne had red hair. Felicity's was longer. Darn. I should have asked Brenda how long the hairs were. Maybe I should text her and ask.

What if Pepper was right, and Felicity had been looking for those ingredients? Nothing had been stolen in the other break-ins. Was that because the burglar wasn't after money or expensive items?

Maybe Jack had been killed because he'd stumbled onto more than just someone trying to break into his shop.

Felicity was rich and wouldn't care about stealing a bank deposit, but maybe she would put the empty envelope there to try to frame Duane. She might have known about the affair if she was lurking around the place. When things went bad, and Jack died by mistake, she would have known the police would take it more seriously, and it would be just like her to try to set someone else up to take the fall.

How else would the bank deposit pouch have gotten in Duane's trash? He certainly wouldn't put it there if he had an alibi and wasn't the killer.

But again, if Pepper's theory was right about all of this having magical origins, then it wasn't out of the question that Felicity had put some kind of spell on Gus. And if Felicity knew that Gus wasn't going to investigate thoroughly, why try to frame Duane? Unless she was afraid Striker might pick up the slack. Was that why Felicity insisted on talking to Striker? Maybe she was planning on putting a hex on him too.

Too bad I couldn't have gotten Gus to drink Elspeth's tea. If drinking something could cure her, did it then stand to reason that drinking something had caused her lack of enthusiasm in the first place?

I thought briefly about the image of the martini glass with the lipstick on the rim that I'd seen in my paper-weight. Maybe that *was* a clue after all. A clue as to why Gus was acting the way she was.

My mind raced. It was looking more and more possible that the break-ins had been about that pleas-antry charm all along. I pulled out my phone, eager to call Striker or my sister, but then they were both busy. I needed to get more information, more proof to support my claims. I pulled out the card Felicity had left the other day for Striker and typed in a text from my phone, pretending to be Striker and asking her to meet at Last Chance Books, then hit Send.

Seconds later I got a response from Felicity.

I'll be there in half an hour and I'll give you my alibi.

24

P andora snuck out of the bookstore through her escape route in the closet shortly after Jack's ghost appeared. Willa was busy talking to him, and when she talked to ghosts, she tended not to notice what was going on around her. It was the perfect cover. She hated sneaking around behind her human's back, but the work of the cats was of the utmost importance, and they had called an emergency meeting.

When she trotted into Elspeth's barn, the discussions were already underway. Otis was sitting in the center of the circle, his chest puffed out with importance.

"I'm telling you, Fluff is investigating this on his own," Otis said.

"But how effective is that, really?" Sasha asked, narrowing her Siamese blue gaze on him. "That human of his thinks she's the cat's meow, and I doubt she'd listen to anything he had to say."

"Don't be so quick to write off his suspicions," Pandora said, moving in beside Otis. She couldn't believe she was about to support her nemesis, but then, stranger things had happened lately. "When I left the bookshop just now, my human was speaking with Jack's ghost. He said he remembered a cat matching Fluff's description lurking around behind his shop the night he died."

Otis gave Pandora some serious side-eye then said, "See? I knew I was correct!"

A murmur of purrs, growls, and meows rose from the other cats in the room as their excitement grew. Finally, perhaps they had the clue they'd been searching for that proved Felicity was indeed Jack's killer.

But then Inkspot, ever the voice of reason, stepped in. "Don't be so hasty. Where you see one, you may not see the other."

Otis scoffed. "You mean that just because Fluff was there doesn't mean Felicity was too? Seems unlikely to me. They stick together, those two."

"Not always." Inkspot straightened and gave the smaller cat a serious stare. "We know that Felicity Bates is after the ingredients to reverse the pleasantry charm, yes. But murder is a whole other ball of yarn."

"Well, that discounts his entire theory, then," Sasha

said, giving an imperious swish to her tail. "A cat couldn't have shot Jack McDougall."

"Yeah!" Snowball chimed in. "We don't have opposable thumbs."

"Indeed." Inkspot nodded. "But it seems Willa might be digging too close to the truth. We don't want her to end up like poor Jack."

"What else is she supposed to do?" Pandora meowed, indignant. "Gus won't do her job, so my human feels she must take justice into her own hands."

"What about the potion?" Kelly asked. "Elspeth made an antidote. Has Gus taken it?"

"Not yet, I don't think," Pandora said. "Last I saw, she took it back to her office with her. And since Willa is still working on the case alone, I'd say not."

"Perhaps we should focus on getting Gus to drink the tea, then," Inkspot said, his deep baritone booming through the shadows in the barn. "We need her to be back to her old self so we can guide her toward arresting the guilty party."

Pandora sighed, searching for a new solution. "Let me try first. I might be able to persuade her. I had some luck earlier getting her to take action."

"Fine. Very good, then," Inkspot said, dismissing them all with a nod. "And, Pandora, protect your human. Felicity Bates can be very dangerous. If she is the killer, Willa might not be safe."

25

A s I waited for Felicity to show up, I tried to stay busy by cataloguing books. It was no use. I was on pins and needles. I kept glancing at the dark windows of Jack's Cards and wondering if inviting Felicity to the bookshop under false pretenses had been a big mistake.

I had no proof that Felicity was involved. Just a gut feeling. Gus and Striker would want something more concrete. Like long red hairs found at the scene. I whipped off a quick text to Brenda, asking about the length of the red hairs she'd found.

No sooner had I sent the text than Felicity arrived with Fluff in his harness. I was standing behind the counter and glanced around the shop to make sure there wouldn't be a cat fight between Fluff and Pandora, but Pandora wasn't in her bed. Probably hiding. Smart kitty.

"Where's Eddie?" Felicity asked without preamble.

"He'll be here," I said. Not a lie exactly. I did expect Striker to show up at some point since he would be getting off work soon and should have seen my text from earlier. "While we wait for him, why don't you tell me what you've really been doing around town?"

Felicity gave me a belligerent look. "I don't have to tell you anything, Willa Chance."

"No, you don't. That's true." I leaned against the counter, grateful for it as a barrier between me and my enemy. Luckily. "I'm guessing you probably killed Jack by accident. If you confess now, you'll get a lighter sentence."

"What?" Felicity scrunched her nose. "I didn't kill anybody. Least of all Jack."

I chuckled. "Nice try. I already know your little Fluff here was at the lamp shop. Gus has proof."

"Lamp shop? What's that got to do with the murder?"

"The burglar broke into both places. Stands to reason the same person's responsible for both. Plus, I happen to know that you asked Jack if you could sniff around in his basement." Oops, maybe I shouldn't have said that, considering I'd heard that from Jack's ghost and wouldn't be able to explain how I'd obtained that information to anyone.

"Really?" Felicity shook her head, sending her bright-red curls bouncing, her expression unimpressed. "Did you ever consider that maybe the robberies and the killing were unrelated?"

"Of course." I squared my shoulders. Actually, I hadn't really considered that. Darn it. Was it true? Probably not. Felicity Bates was a liar. Everyone knew that. Felicity had something to do with all this. I just knew it. I raised my chin. "But really. What are the odds they aren't related? I mean, you do have a history of untruths. And who's to say you haven't killed before... then blamed it on your son."

Those were fighting words. I knew it. But I needed to get a rise out of her to make her tell me the truth.

Felicity's green eyes sparkled with outrage and fury. "How dare you? I've never killed anyone in my life. Eddie isn't coming, is he? Which makes you the liar here, Willa, not me. You coerced me here under false pretenses to try and get a lame confession out of me. Well, it won't work because I'm not guilty!"

I crossed my arms over my chest and gave her a pointed look. "So *you* say. Why do you want to see Striker so badly anyway? Are you planning to hex him, too, so he can't investigate?"

She leaned in over the counter, and I took a step back. She could be frightful when she wanted to. "You listen to me, Wilhelmina Chance. There are things going on here that you know nothing about. Big things. Important things. There is more at stake here than your little brain can fathom, and if you know what is good for you, then you will mind your own business and let your sister do the police work."

Before I could say anything else, she stormed out of my shop, taking her cat with her.

Darn it. I'd probably just blown my best shot at solving the case, and I shouldn't have provoked her the way that I had, but she was my best lead. If only Gus wasn't being so lackadaisical about everything, I wouldn't have to be so vigilant. Trying to investigate on my own really wasn't easy. I needed my sister.

The bells above the door jangled once more and drew me out of my funk. It was the bartender from the Blue Moon, there to collect the book she'd ordered.

"Hey," she said, smiling. "Thanks for staying open late for me."

"You're welcome." I pulled out the book from under the counter and handed it to her. "You prepaid, so you're all set."

"Thanks." The bartender cocked her head, glancing out the front windows then back to me. "I saw your sister's girlfriend on the way in here. She seemed upset. Did you guys have a fight?"

"Girlfriend?" The word stopped me short. "Oh, she's not Gus's friend."

"Really?" She shrugged. "Huh. They've been pretty chummy, hanging out at the Blue Moon."

"You must be mistaken." I shook my head. "My sister can't stand Felicity Bates."

"If you say so." The bartender started back toward the front door. "But judging on the number of drinks Felicity's been buying for Gus, I'd say there's definitely something there."

My eyes widened. I came around the counter to stand before her. "She's been buying my sister drinks?"

"Sure. While Gus is playing piano, usually. Felicity orders them at the bar then delivers them herself during your sister's set. She did it for three nights in a row one time, but not the past couple of nights. Gus hasn't been there since the night before they discovered Jack's murder. Apparently she's been working on the case."

Alarm bells went off inside my head. "You're saying Gus was at the Blue Moon the night of the murder? All night?"

"Yep." The bartender gave me a funny look. "I figured you already knew that. She was there from open to close. And Jack's body wasn't discovered until the next morning, so Gus didn't have to rush out for a call or anything. Felicity was there all night too."

Stunned, I leaned a hand against the back of one of the armchairs as the bartender walked out. Gus had been at the Blue Moon. Felicity had been at the Blue Moon. Duane had been at the Blue Moon. Was the whole town hanging out there? And the fact that they were there until closing meant that neither Felicity nor Duane could be the killer.

Then who *was* the killer? And were the break-ins related or something separate as Felicity had suggested? And how in the world had Felicity and Gus become friends?

It was closing time. The shop proprietors were starting to lock up and go home. I supposed I should do the same. Maybe I could puzzle things out with Striker, or maybe Jack's ghost would make an appearance and have something more enlightening.

Glancing down the street, I spied activity by Jack's card shop. No, it wasn't his shop. It was the Crosbys' ice cream store. Anne was at the door, apparently locking up for the night. She looked better today, wearing makeup and the red lipstick, which I was now sure would match the smear on Jack's collar. She glanced around as if making sure no one could see her and hurried down the street, pulling the lavender shawl I'd seen in her knitting bag tight around her to ward off the chill.

Now, that was odd behavior. She was walking fast, as if running from something, and there was something else.

The shawl.

I closed my eyes, thinking back to the talk I'd had with Duane and Anne in their shop. Duane had pointed to the knitting bag and mentioned that she'd been knitting that shawl for the class, using that to illustrate how Mrs. Quimby's memory wasn't always correct and her statement that she'd seen him there near the time of Jack's death was not to be believed.

But when I'd been in Mrs. Quimby's shop the other day, the flyer said they were knitting socks, and Brenda even had a sock in her bag.

Anne had a motive to kill Jack—he'd just broken up with her. Anne had red hair, and Brenda had found red hair by the back door. Anne would have been angry over the breakup, and she had seemed overly upset that day I talked to her and Duane. What if Anne had left Jack's after he broke things off, just as his ghost had said, but then came back and broke in through the back door later on to kill him.

She might have been trying to make it look like it was tied into the break-ins. That could also explain why his deposit pouch was in the trash bin that went with the Crosbys' store. Perhaps she didn't realize that nothing was stolen from the other break-ins and took it to throw the police off track and make them assume Jack's break-in was connected to the others.

Anne had no alibi. She and Duane had both claimed to be home, but later on, Duane confessed he was at the Blue Moon, so there was no one to verify that Anne really was home during the time of the murder.

I grabbed the key to my store, locked up, and rushed

out into the street. I had to catch Anne and question her about that night. Maybe I could catch her in a mistake that Gus could use to get her to confess.

She must have turned in to a side street because I couldn't see her. Darn.

I rushed down the street, craning my neck to see across, searching for a glimpse of the lavender shawl. I stayed on my side of the street, thinking that I would have a wider view of the street opposite where Anne was. I was so intent on looking for her, that I wasn't paying attention to the path in front of me—

"Ooof!"

I spun around, catching Mrs. Quimby just before she fell backward. I'd practically knocked her over.

"Willa! What in the world is your hurry?" She held her tall iced coffee away from her body as the liquid and ice cubes inside swirled. Good thing the cup had a lid, or she would have been wearing it.

I briefly wondered about the wisdom of a woman her age having caffeine this late or even drinking iced coffee in this chilly weather, but my concern for her welfare after I'd practically run her down took precedence. "I'm so sorry. Are you okay?"

She paused for a second, as if taking an internal assessment, then smiled. "Yes, dear, but you really must be more careful."

"I know. I'm sorry." My gaze drifted over to the other

side of the street again. Anne was nowhere in sight. Then I realized Mrs. Quimby might have some of the answers I needed.

"Well then, I was just closing up, so I'll be on my way." She started down the street.

"Before you go, I have a question about the knitting class," I said. "The one on the night Jack was killed."

She turned back toward me, her blue eyes narrowing slightly. "Yes?"

"Do you remember if Anne Crosby was there?"

"Of course, didn't I already tell you that?" She sounded annoyed. "Honestly, people talk about my memory. You're much too young to be that forgetful."

"It's just that I thought the class project was a pair of socks, but Anne claimed she made a shawl." It wasn't exactly Anne who had claimed that. It was Duane. But Anne hadn't disagreed, so I figured it was close enough.

Mrs. Quimby's gaze darted to the shop window, where I could see the flyer for the class was posted. It clearly said the project was a pair of socks. She straightened, looking offended. "We don't always stick to the announced project. We like to go with the flow. I don't see what this has to do with anything."

Now I felt bad. She was clearly insulted. "Oh, I was just wondering. I didn't mean anything by it."

"Are you working for your sister?" The ice cubes in

her drink clanked together, drawing my eye to the tumbler.

"No. Well, sort of." If she thought I was working for Gus, would that cause her to open up more? I hoped so. "So Anne did knit that shawl the night of the class?"

"Yes, and she chose a lovely lavender yarn too."

"Did Anne go straight to her car when class let out? Or maybe she went across to the ice cream shop?"

We both glanced over at the shop, which was now closed, its windows dark. Beside it, the yellow crime scene tape fluttered in Jack's doorway.

"No... I told you everyone left. I only saw Jack and Duane over there."

"Wasn't that the night you couldn't find your car? Maybe you saw her when you were looking for it."

She scowled. "No, I already told you that wasn't the night. It's not like I lose my car every night."

"But Brenda McDougall drove you around to find your car that night and then followed you home," I said.

She frowned as if puzzled, and my worry increased. Maybe Mrs. Quimby's memory was worse than I thought. But her shrewd blue eyes were clear as day. She chuckled almost to herself. "Oh, that's right. That *was* the night Brenda drove me around, looking for my car. Silly me. Got home a little later than usual that night, around ten thirty. But I didn't see Anne running around that night. Is that important?"

"I'm not sure. Maybe."

"Well, then, if there is nothing else, I will just go home. I'd like to get there before my shows are all over." She gave me a sour look, apparently to discourage me from asking more questions that might keep her from her shows, then turned and headed down the street to her car. When she got there, she glanced back at me. It was then I noticed a group of short white hairs had escaped from her bun and were sticking out in all directions. She put her iced coffee on the roof, unlocked the car, retrieved the iced coffee, and got inside.

As I watched her drive away, an unsettling feeling came over me. What if I'd been all wrong about this whole thing from the start? I rushed back to my store. If my suspicions were correct, then I needed to talk to either Gus or Striker right away.

B ack at the shop, I collapsed on the couch. I hadn't
gotten any messages from Gus, Striker, or Brenda.
I supposed I didn't really need Brenda's answer about the
red hairs. Felicity couldn't be the killer. She'd been with
Gus at the time of the murder.

"This is all so confusing!" I said aloud, even though I
was alone. Speaking of that, where was Pandora? I
usually talked out my clues with her, but she wasn't in
her cat bed or on any of the other furniture. Maybe she'd
found a nice corner to snooze in, uninterrupted. I was
too tired to look for her. She would come out sooner or
later.

Robert Frost and Franklin Pierce appeared from
between the shelves, staring at me quizzically. Guess I
wasn't totally alone.

"Why so glum?" Robert asked me before turning to Franklin. "She does look glum, doesn't she?"

"I'm not glum. I'm thinking," I said. "This case is driving me nuts. Too many suspects, and the person I really want to be guilty couldn't have done it." I sank back against the cushions, dejected.

"Maybe it will help you to talk it out," Robert suggested.

"Yeah," Franklin agreed. "Who are your suspects?"

"Well, there's Anne Crosby. She was having an affair with Jack, and he broke things off that night."

"Oh dear," Franklin said as he and Robert exchanged startled looks. "A crime of passion!"

"Maybe," I said. "Anne was at the knitting class earlier that night. She must have gone to the shop for their rendezvous, and Jack broke it off. But the class got out at nine, and Jack was killed around ten, so she didn't have much time to think about it. I mean, it probably took a while to have the breakup conversation."

"Usually does," Franklin said knowingly.

"Then she probably got mad, grabbed the gun, shot him, and fled." I glanced toward the windows, where I could barely see the corner of Jack's shop. "If she went out the front, someone would have seen her, so she must have gone out the back."

Robert nodded. "Many a poem has been written about such things."

"There's one thing that strikes me as odd, though," I said. "If Anne is the killer, it seems likely she would have been blinded by anger. Would she have had the presence of mind to take the deposit envelope and the money?"

"That does seem rather calculated," Franklin said. "Perhaps it wasn't her. Who else have you got?"

I let my head fall back so I was staring up at the ceiling. I really didn't want to voice my suspicions of the kind, elderly yarn-shop owner out loud, but at least Franklin and Robert wouldn't be able to tell anyone. "There's Mrs. Quimby, who owns the yarn shop."

Robert looked surprised. "That nice old lady who comes in for the knitting books?"

"Yep. I actually didn't suspect her until just now. But there was something odd about the conversation we just had. This whole time, I'd been hoping the culprit was Felicity Bates. I'm even willing to believe that Pepper was right about all of this having magical origins. Now I know Felicity can't be the killer, but what if it really does have magical origins?"

"What do you mean?" Franklin looked completely onboard with the break-ins and murder being magically motivated. I guessed he would have to believe in the supernatural now that he was a ghost.

"If someone is going around looking for the ingredients to reverse the pleasantry charm, it stands to reason they might have put some sort of spell on Gus so she wouldn't investigate. And if Elspeth's tea is some sort of antidote, then that means Elspeth might be magical. And if a drink could reverse whatever spell was on Gus, then maybe a drink is what caused it."

"Not following you, Willa." Franklin turned to Robert. "Are you?"

Robert shook his head.

"I saw Mrs. Quimby give Gus an iced coffee the other day, and I seem to recall Gus saying she had tea with Mrs. Quimby when she was questioning her about the case." I sat up straighter on the couch. "What if Mrs. Quimby is magical, too, and put a spell or hex on Gus?"

"Just because she gave her beverages?" Robert didn't look convinced. "That's kind of stretching it."

I shook my head. "It's not just that. A whiteish-blond hair was found at the scene of one of the break-ins. Everyone assumed it was human, but I thought it might be from Fluff. Of course, that was when Felicity was my main suspect. I even mentioned it to Gus, and she laughed at me. Maybe that was because the hair really is human."

Franklin tsked. "How rude of her to laugh at you, though."

Robert still wasn't convinced. "Mrs. Quimby has short white hair. But surely giving Gus a coffee and having short white hair isn't enough?"

"No, there's something else. Just now, I ran into her

out in the street, and she acted odd when I asked about the night Jack died. I was trying to find out if she'd seen Anne running out of Jack's or something because earlier Brenda had said Mrs. Quimby had lost her car and Brenda helped her find it. But Mrs. Quimby insisted she didn't lose her car, then suddenly it seemed like she all of a sudden agreed with me."

"Why would she do that?" Franklin asked.

"To create an alibi," Robert offered.

Franklin pondered that a moment. "So, if Mrs. Quimby is the killer, and she was after the ingredients for the charm, then why would she take the deposit money?"

"Maybe Mrs. Quimby's mind isn't slipping like we think it is. She could be cleverly playing the fool. She might have taken the deposit envelope to throw the police off track."

"So, then, how did it end up in the Crosbys' trash?" Robert asked.

"Good question." I thought about that.

"And why didn't the police find it?" Franklin asked.

"They probably didn't look in Duane's trash, just Jack's," I said. "And Brenda probably didn't look in there either."

"But why would Mrs. Quimby put it in there in the first place?" Robert asked.

"Well, if she was lying about losing her car that night,

then she could have seen Anne and..." I let my voice trail off, something niggling at the back of my brain.

"And..." Robert prompted.

I shot up from the couch. "I think I know who the killer is!"

"Me too!" Franklin tried to snap his ghostly fingers, but they just passed through each other. "It could only be... ruh-roh!"

He and Robert disappeared in a flash just as the bells over the door chimed.

I jerked my head around in time to see the newcomer turn the sign to closed and pull the shade.

The good news was that I'd correctly guessed who the killer was. The bad news was she was pointing a gun right at my chest.

27

Pandora had left Elspeth's barn and raced as fast as she could to the sheriff's department. Luckily she was able to sneak in the front door when a patrolman opened it, as there was no time to waste. She made a beeline to Gus's office.

Gus and Jimmy were in there, going over clues. That was good news. At least Gus was working. Jimmy had written a bunch of clues on the whiteboard and was pointing at them with the capped marker.

Pandora's hopes were dashed, however, when Gus picked up her own marker and drew a tic-tac-toe board. She put a big X in the corner and handed the pen to Jimmy. "Your turn."

Jimmy hesitated then took the pen. "Is this going to help us figure out the killer?"

Gus shrugged. "Sure. Beats going over the clues again and again."

Jimmy nodded slowly. "I see. You have a secret method that you're not letting on. Well, fine, I'll play." He put a big O in the center.

This wouldn't do at all. Gus was no closer to investigating than she had been earlier. She certainly hadn't ingested Elspeth's antidote tea. Pandora's only hope was that she hadn't tossed it out.

As she looked around the room, relief spread through her when she saw the tumbler on Gus's desk. Now to get her to drink it. Pandora jumped up on the corner of the desk, causing both Gus and Jimmy to jump. Apparently neither of them had noticed her come in. Pandora's chest puffed out. She took great pride in her stealth entrances.

Normally, she would expect Gus to shoo her away and get mad before throwing her out, but not today. Gus scooted her chair over closer and scratched Pandora behind the ears.

"Well, hi there, little friend. How did you get all the way over here?" Gus asked.

"Is that your sister's cat?" Jimmy asked. "The one that hangs around in the bookstore?"

"Yep." Gus moved her scratching down Pandora's back, and Pandora let out a purr. "She's smarter than Willa thinks, aren't you?"

Yep. Pandora meowed her agreement then flopped on her side so Gus could scratch a different area. Jimmy joined in, and Pandora twitched her tail in pleasure, hitting something metal and cold. Oh, right. The tumbler. Remembering her mission, Pandora rolled back to a sitting position and pushed the cup toward Gus.

Gus pushed it out of the way and continued the petting.

Darn. Pandora would have to come up with another tactic to get the human to drink the tea. She closed her eyes and concentrated all of her feline powers on Gus, willing her to drink.

It took a few minutes to work, but soon Gus's petting slowed down, and she looked around the desk. Pandora held her breath as Gus's eyes fell on the tumbler.

Almost there... now drink!

Finally, Gus reached out for the cup. Pandora let out a triumphant meow.

Gus made a face. "Huh. That's probably spoiled by now. Best throw it out so I don't get sick."

No! Pandora meowed loudly and lunged between Gus's hand and the cup. Gus had misunderstood her communication. She tried one last time, focusing all her energy on getting the human to guzzle the drink down before all was lost.

28

B renda McDougall glared at me, the gun steady in her hand. "Were you talking to someone? I don't think so because I've been watching your door, and no one else is in the shop."

I swallowed hard, staring at the gun pointed at my chest. "Uh, no one. I wasn't talking to anyone. I'm here alone."

Brenda laughed. "If you're talking to yourself, maybe you're crazy. Probably dumb as your sister too. Too bad you weren't dumb enough to let my husband's case go. I'm afraid you stuck your nose in too deep." She waved the gun around as she talked. "Looks like another one of the Mystic Notch robberies will end up in a death."

"I don't know what you're talking about," I hedged, praying that Striker would miraculously show up or something. "I don't know anything about the case. I was just sitting here, reading, and—"

"Stop it! Stop lying." Brenda glared at me. "I know you're investigating. Otherwise why text me about the red hairs? They were short, by the way. Yeah. I know all about him and Anne Crosby. Cheater deserved what he got."

"So, you shot him because he was cheating?" I asked, stalling. "Why not just divorce him?"

"What? And split all the money with him? No way. Besides, I wanted it all for myself." She snorted. "Then those break-ins came along and gave me the perfect cover."

At my surprised look, she shook her head. "No. The break-ins weren't me, but I did take advantage of them. And I was the one who planted the idea in Jack's head that he should hide in the store to try and catch whoever was doing it."

"So, he did what you suggested, and then what?" Keeping her monologuing would give me more time to figure a way out of this mess, I hoped.

"Then I went in and shot him." Brenda shrugged, acting more like she was describing a trip to the grocery store than retelling the murder of her husband. "I knew where he kept the gun, of course. I came to visit him after closing time and found him sitting in that chair, asleep. He never knew what hit him."

Her flat tone made me shiver. Fear fizzed inside me like soda pop, ready to explode, but I had to stay focused if I wanted to survive. I kept her talking. "What about the deposit?"

"Oh, that." Brenda gave a dismissive wave of her free hand, the gun still trained on me with the other. "I took the envelope to make it look like a robbery. The idea to set Duane up for it occurred to me later. Would've worked too. Then you had to go and stick your big nose into things."

"So, when you were spotted skulking around the trash bins, it wasn't to find clues. You were planting the envelope in Duane's trash can?" At least I'd been right about that. Too bad I hadn't figured it out until the end of my conversation with Franklin and Robert.

"Yep." Brenda looked pleased with herself.

"But how did you pull it off? If you followed Mrs. Quimby home that night, how did you get back by ten?"

Brenda's laugh set my nerves on edge. "That was brilliant, if I do say so myself. Mrs. Quimby's memory issues played right into my plan. You see, I knew she had forgotten where she parked her car once, so I took her keys from the hook on the door, moved her car, then put the keys back. Of course she just thought I was in the shop getting yarn. Then later that night, I came back just in time to see her standing on the street where her car had been with a confused look on her face. Naturally I offered to help her find her car and follow her home."

"Okay, but that still doesn't explain the timing."

"That's the brilliant part. It wasn't the night I killed Jack that I helped her find her car, it was the week before. I knew with her memory issues, I could easily convince folks—and possibly even Mrs. Q herself—that it was the night of Jack's murder that I'd followed her home."

"Sneaky," I said. "So that night you went straight from the knitting class to the card shop and shot Jack?"

"Not exactly. I actually didn't even go to the knitting class. Couldn't face that tramp, Anne Crosby." She made a disgusted face.

I realized I'd made a fatal error of assumption. When I'd seen the lavender shawl in Anne's bag, I'd assumed that it was Anne who hadn't attended the knitting class, but it had really been Brenda who didn't attend. She hadn't known that the class project had changed from socks to a shawl and had knitted the sock as part of her cover story.

"Anyway, I was waiting until all the shops were closed, and I saw that tramp, Anne, go over. I thought I'd have to give up and try to kill him another night, but she came out quicker than I thought. Guess things didn't take so long that night. I waited for a bit because I happened to know that Jack would fall asleep right away, and then I snuck in and grabbed the gun."

"And shot him before he even knew what was happening."

"Yeah." She smiled at her own cleverness, then her face snapped back into its previous angry expression. She stepped closer and shoved the gun in my face. "But you asked too many questions, and when I saw you talking to Mrs. Quimby, I knew I had to get rid of you before you spoiled everything. Now get moving to the back of the store."

As we walked, I could hear her knocking things off the shelves behind me. My heart raced. She was going to stage things to look like another robbery. I needed a plan and quickly diverted my steps to lead her past the presidential biography section.

"Hey. Wait a minute. Where do you think you're going? This place needs to look messier. Help me pull some more of those books off the shelf..." She pointed the gun toward the Franklin Pierce biographies and tugged on a book, then froze, frowning and looking around her. "Do you feel that? It's really cold!"

I seized my opportunity and tackled her to the floor. We rolled around between the shelves, both fighting for control of the gun. I glanced up and saw Franklin and Robert hovering over us, cheering me on.

"Kick her in the shin, Willa! She knocked down my memoir!" Franklin yelled.

I rolled to the right and tried to kick, but my old leg injury flared up, causing me to lose my grip on her.

"Aha!" She gained the advantage, jumping on top of me.

"Punch her in the jaw!" Robert swirled around the bookshelf, tugging at one of the books. Meanwhile, Brenda was trying to get ahold of my wrists with one hand, presumably so she could pin me down and shoot me. I squirmed and struggled, all the while watching Robert as he tugged on the book.

The book inched out. Brenda pinned my right hand down with her left hand, but she was holding the gun in her right. I swung up with my left hand just as the book Robert was tugging on teetered at the edge of the shelf.

Bam!

The book fell on Brenda's head, and she let go of my wrist and slouched forward. "Ouch!"

I was just prying Brenda's fingers off the gun when a loud crash sounded from the front of the door, and footsteps raced toward us.

"Hands up or I'll shoot!" Gus said. "And I don't care who I hit!"

Brenda and I both halted and did as she asked, what with my sister's weapon pointed in our faces and all.

Gus hauled us to our feet and passed Brenda over to

Jimmy, who Mirandized her while slapping handcuffs on her wrists. I brushed off my pants and did my best to calm my thundering pulse just as Striker showed up as well.

My sister gave me a disparaging look and shook her head. "I told you not to butt into my cases, Willa. I know what I'm doing."

Striker caught my gaze, and we both just shrugged. Pandora twined around my ankles, meowing loudly as Jimmy led Brenda out to his waiting squad car. Seemed we would have a happy ending after all.

A few days later, we were all gathered in the seating area at the front of Last Chance Books. My sister was her old self again, and of course, she was still lecturing me about the dangers of butting in on official law-enforcement business. But given how things turned out, I was okay with it.

"And what the hell was that drink you gave me from Elspeth?" Gus asked, her nose wrinkled. "Seriously. It tasted like old socks. You told me it was the stuff she made for us when we were kids, but it certainly was not! I'm not even sure what possessed me to drink it after it had been sitting on my desk for so long. Good thing I didn't get food poisoning. Yuck!"

I snorted. "What's really lucky is that you weren't poisoned from the drinks Felicity was giving you at the Blue Moon."

"Huh?" Gus looked confused. "Felicity Bates gave me drinks? When? I don't even like her. Besides, she's the one who broke into the other shops. No way would I befriend a criminal."

Striker and I exchanged glances. Yep. My sister was definitely back to normal.

"I gave her a fine too," Gus continued. "Couldn't arrest her, unfortunately, since nothing was stolen. Doubted I could make it stick. So, the fine was the best I could do." She shook her head, scowling. "All these rich types. Got nothing better to do. Hopefully there'll be no more shenanigans from her or that other one. Sarah Delaney. You ask me, those two are bad news."

"What do you think about Felicity getting fined?" I asked Striker. I admit I was testing him to see what he would say. The way Felicity kept showing up at the shop and asking for "Eddie" still had me riled up.

"Huh?" He gave me a confused stare.

"Felicity," I repeated. "She told me that she'd only give her alibi to you. Seems pretty friendly to me. How well do you two know each other?"

"Not that well," he said, his hand squeezing mine. "Trust me. I'm guessing she only wanted to talk to me because I'm law enforcement too, and Gus was... well, under the weather. Probably wanted to make sure she didn't get nailed for murder."

"Hmm." It was good to know that he wasn't any

friendlier with Felicity than I'd thought. I still wondered about her motives. Did she want to slip him a potion, or was her interest for another reason? It didn't matter, though. Things were good with me and Striker right now. I leaned over and kissed his cheek. "Okay."

Gus made a face at us. Yep, she was back to her old self.

"So I guess I was right about the white hairs from the break-in at the lamp shop being cat hair," I said. Striker had told me the report had come back from the lab indicating the hair was feline.

Gus narrowed her eyes at me. "Yeah, but don't let that go to your head. It was an easy guess. Who else's white hair would it be?"

Her question brought on a pang of guilt. How could I have suspected Mrs. Quimby?

"Brenda's lie about her following Mrs. Quimby home had me going for a while. What about you?" I asked my sister.

"Nah. I figured she was lying. Mrs. Quimby had sworn she didn't lose her car that night. But then she waffled." Gus looked at me almost as if she'd known that I'd also questioned Mrs. Quimby about that night. I shrank back in my seat a little under her withering stare. "However, I happened to know that Mrs. Quimby often does that. She doesn't want others to know that her memory is bad, so sometimes she just agrees even if she isn't sure that's what really happened."

"Oh, I hope she'll be okay," I said.

"She's fine. Memory issues are common with age, and according to her doctor, hers aren't getting worse," Gus said. "Besides, she's still sharp enough to remember that I like iced coffee with extra sugar."

"I'll be sure to keep an eye on her, make sure she finds her car at night." It was the least I could do, considering how I'd suspected her, even if it was only for a brief moment.

"I need to get back to work," Gus said, pushing to her feet. She stopped at the door and looked back at us. "Willa, I'm telling you, mind your own business. And keep that cat of yours out of my office too."

She left, and Pandora jumped up on the seat between us.

Striker put his arm around me, petting the cat with his other hand. "Looks like we got our old Gus back."

"Yeah," I said, watching my sister walk away outside. "But is that a good or bad thing?"

WHILE STRIKER and Willa talked about the case on the couch, Pandora trotted over to her cat bed to relive her own personal victories of the day. She'd pulled out all the stops to concentrate her full focus on getting Gus to drink the tea. It had taken a few precious minutes, but Gus had eventually grabbed the tumbler and guzzled down the drink. She'd burped afterward, too, which Pandora took to mean the elixir was potent. No surprise there since it had come from Elspeth.

After downing the drink, Gus had turned her attention to the whiteboard. A funny look had come over her face, then she'd grabbed the marker from Jimmy and drawn several lines connecting the clues. Cramming the top on the marker, she'd turned to Jimmy and declared, "It's obvious what happened here and who the killer is!"

Then she'd checked her phone and, upon seeing the message from Willa, had rushed out to the squad car. Pandora could barely keep up with her and just managed to jump into the backseat before Gus took off, with the lights flashing and sirens blaring. On the way to Willa's, they'd met up with Striker coming from Dixville Pass, and he'd followed behind them all the way to the shop.

Once inside, Gus had no problem capturing Brenda. Of course the humans would never give Pandora credit for the vital role she'd played in this whole thing, but she was used to that. The cats of Mystic Notch were rarely recognized for their achievements, but that was okay as long as peace prevailed in the Notch.

Pandora stared out the window, seeing nothing but

empty sidewalks. She'd heard that the fine Gus had levied on Felicity had curtailed her actions. She couldn't very well keep going around breaking into places now that she'd been caught. But Pandora knew that, while Felicity and Fluff might be gone for now, eventually they would be back and searching even harder. The cats would have to be extra vigilant in the days ahead.

Yawning, Pandora turned over to look at Willa and Striker. At least her cat-to-human communication had improved. Maybe not with Willa, but Gus had certainly succumbed to her wishes. Come to think of it, it would be kind of fun to mess with Gus along those lines in the coming weeks. Pandora wondered just how much control she could gain over the stubborn sheriff.

But there would be plenty of time for that after a nice long nap. Pandora's eyes grew heavy, and she drifted off to sleep, barely noticing the clump of fluffy white fur stuck to the side of her cat bed.

****

Sign up for my newsletter and get my latest releases at the lowest discount price, plus I'll send you a free copy of *Dead Wrong*, book 1 in the award winning paranormal Blackmoore Sisters Paranormal Cozy Mystery Series: https://mystic_notch.gr8.com/

Books in the Mystic Notch series:

Ghostly Paws
A Spirited Tail
A Mew To A Kill
Paws and Effect
Probable Paws
A Whisker of a Doubt
Wrong Side of the Claw

If you want to receive a text message on your cell phone when I have a new release, text COZYMYSTERY to 88202 (sorry, this only works for US cell phones!)

Join my readers group on Facebook:
https://www.facebook.com/groups/ldobbsreaders

MORE BOOKS BY LEIGHANN DOBBS:

Cozy Mysteries

Silver Hollow
Paranormal Cozy Mystery Series
***

A Spell of Trouble (Book 1)
Spell Disaster (Book 2)
Nothing to Croak About (Book 3)
Cry Wolf (Book 4)
Shear Magic (Book 5)

Blackmoore Sisters

Cozy Mystery Series

* * *

Dead Wrong

Dead & Buried

Dead Tide

Buried Secrets

Deadly Intentions

A Grave Mistake

Spell Found

Fatal Fortune

Hidden Secrets

Mystic Notch
Cat Cozy Mystery Series

* * *

Ghostly Paws

A Spirited Tail

A Mew To A Kill

Paws and Effect

Probable Paws

Whisker of a Doubt

Wrong Side of the Claw

Oyster Cove Guesthouse

Cat Cozy Mystery Series
***

A Twist in the Tail
A Whisker in the Dark

Kate Diamond Mystery Adventures
***

Hidden Agemda (Book 1)
Ancient Hiss Story (Book 2)
Heist Society (Book 3)

Mooseamuck Island
Cozy Mystery Series
* * *

A Zen For Murder
A Crabby Killer
A Treacherous Treasure

Lexy Baker
Cozy Mystery Series
* * *

Lexy Baker Cozy Mystery Series Boxed Set Vol 1 (Books 1-4)

Or buy the books separately:

Killer Cupcakes
Dying For Danish
Murder, Money and Marzipan
3 Bodies and a Biscotti
Brownies, Bodies & Bad Guys
Bake, Battle & Roll
Wedded Blintz
Scones, Skulls & Scams
Ice Cream Murder
Mummified Meringues
Brutal Brulee (Novella)
No Scone Unturned
Cream Puff Killer
Never Say Pie

Lady Katherine Regency Mysteries
***

An Invitation to Murder (Book 1)
The Baffling Burglaries of Bath (Book 2)
Murder at the Ice Ball (Book 3)
A Murderous Affair (Book 4)

Hazel Martin Historical Mystery Series
***

Murder at Lowry House (book 1)
Murder by Misunderstanding (book 2)

Sam Mason Mysteries
(As L. A. Dobbs)
***

Telling Lies (Book 1)
Keeping Secrets (Book 2)
Exposing Truths (Book 3)
Betraying Trust (Book 4)
Killing Dreams (Book 5)

Romantic Comedy
***

Corporate Chaos Series

In Over Her Head (book 1)
Can't Stand the Heat (book 2)
What Goes Around Comes Around (book 3)
Careful What You Wish For (4)

Contemporary Romance
***

More Books By Leighann Dobbs:

Reluctant Romance

Sweet Romance (Written As Annie Dobbs)
Firefly Inn Series
❋❋❋

Another Chance (Book 1)
Another Wish (Book 2)

Hometown Hearts Series
❋❋❋

No Getting Over You (Book 1)
A Change of Heart (Book 2)

Sweet Mountain Billionaires
❋❋❋

Jaded Billionaire (Book 1)
A Billion Reasons Not To Fall In Love (Book 2)

———

Regency Romance
❋ ❋ ❋

Scandals and Spies Series:

Kissing The Enemy
Deceiving the Duke
Tempting the Rival
Charming the Spy
Pursuing the Traitor
Captivating the Captain

ABOUT THE AUTHOR

USA Today best-selling Author, Leighann Dobbs, has had a passion for reading since she was old enough to hold a book, but she didn't put pen to paper until much later in life. After a twenty-year career as a software engineer, with a few side trips into selling antiques and making jewelry, she realized you can't make a living reading books, so she tried her hand at writing them and discovered she had a passion for that, too! She lives in New Hampshire with her husband, Bruce, their trusty Chihuahua mix, Mojo, and beautiful rescue cat, Kitty.

Find out about her latest books and how to get discounts on them by signing up at:
    https://mystic_notch.gr8.com/

If you want to receive a text message alert on your cell phone for new releases , text COZYMYSTERY to 88202 (sorry, this only works for US cell phones!)

Connect with Leighann on Facebook
    http://facebook.com/leighanndobbsbooks

This is a work of fiction.

None of it is real. All names, places, and events are products of the
author's imagination. Any resemblance to real names, places, or events
are purely coincidental, and should not be construed as being real.

Made in the USA
Columbia, SC
10 June 2024

36904358R00128